Chapter 1

I felt different today, and I didn't know why.

Was it that I was wrapped in a little girl's princess comforter and matching pink sheets? Was it the always-present warmth that filled Lily's house? For some reason, I felt younger. Watched over. Part of my best friend's family.

I liked the feeling.

I snuggled under Lily's little sister's comforter, as the morning sun poked through the eyelet-lace curtains and formed kaleidoscope patterns on the walls. Every window in the Randazzos' huge Victorian house was draped with the same curtains. Lily hated them. Too frilly. Not cool. But I liked how the curtains were all alike. They made the big house cozy.

So unlike my own house.

My house creaked with strange noises. The air hung damp and chilly, and, although Dad and Lady Azura were always there with me, it never felt cozy, because we were never alone. There were others. Some came and went, while others lingered. Not everyone could see them, but I always knew they were there.

You might be wondering who they were.

Ghosts.

"Do you know what I'm thinking?" Lily asked, her long, dark hair falling in a tangle around her face. Her big brown eyes glinted mischievously at me from across the room.

"No." I stifled a yawn. We'd stayed up really late talking. Mostly about Jayden, my sort of, kind of first boyfriend, who had moved back to Atlanta. Did that make him my ex-boyfriend? I had wondered. But according to Lily, since Jayden and I were never *officially* going out, we never officially broke up when he moved. We just sort of said good-bye and promised to keep in touch. We'd been texting off and on, but it wasn't the same. Lily was convinced I'd meet a new boy in no time . . . she managed to change her crushes practically weekly . . . but I wasn't so sure. It had taken

SARANORMAL

The Secrets Within

by Phoebe Rivers

SIMON SPOTLIGHT
New York London Toronto Sydney New Delhi

This book is a work of fiction. Any references to historical events, real people, or real places are used fictitiously. Other names, characters, places, and events are products of the author's imagination, and any resemblance to actual events or places or persons, living or dead, is entirely coincidental.

SIMON SPOTLIGHT
An imprint of Simon & Schuster Children's Publishing Division
1230 Avenue of the Americas, New York, New York 10020
Copyright © 2013 by Simon & Schuster, Inc.
All rights reserved, including the right of reproduction in whole or in part in any form.
SIMON SPOTLIGHT and colophon are registered trademarks of Simon & Schuster, Inc.
Text by Heather Alexander
For information about special discounts for bulk purchases, please contact Simon & Schuster
Special Sales at 1-866-506-1949 or business@simonandschuster.com.
Manufactured in the United States of America 0313 OFF
First Edition 10 9 8 7 6 5 4 3 2 1
ISBN 978-1-4424-6849-8 (pbk)
ISBN 978-1-4424-6850-4 (hc)
ISBN 978-1-4424-6851-1 (eBook)

Library of Congress Catalog Card Number 2012941867

me twelve years to meet one Jayden. What were the odds I'd meet another one anytime soon?

I pushed myself up and faced Lily, who was stretching in her bed. Lily's four-year-old sister, Cammie, gave me her bed whenever I slept over. She always made a big drama of it, but I knew Cammie was secretly thrilled. My bed takeover was the perfect excuse to spend the night tucked between her parents.

"Come on," Lily scoffed. "You so know what I'm thinking, Sara." She raised her thick eyebrows and gave me a knowing stare.

I gulped. I'd thought we were done with that. "I don't know."

"Try harder," Lily coaxed. "Focus."

"I can't do *that* anymore," I protested. "The mind reading was a one-time thing. Really," I insisted. "I hate talking about this."

"Whoa!" Lily raised her arms in protest. "I was totally not going there. I was just thinking how we should challenge my lame little brothers to a pancake-eating contest. That's all."

"Oh." Color flamed my cheeks. I felt heat rise around my ears.

Lily swung her legs onto the floor. "You should trust me. I mean, I promised to never mention the mind reading, right?"

"I'm sorry," I said lamely. And I was. Truly. Lily had been my best friend ever since I'd moved to Stellamar last year. She'd stuck by me through a lot of weird stuff and never questioned me. I knew she was the real deal. Lily was loyal and never judged me. "You always keep promises," I told her. "I'm just really tired. And hungry. I bet I can down more pancakes than you."

"You're on!" Lily hurried out the door with me at her heels. And like that, my weirdness was forgotten. As always.

Recently, right before my birthday, she'd figured out I could read people's minds. She'd seen it happen, right before her eyes. I avoided talking about it, hoping and praying she hadn't put it all together . . . but she had, of course. When she finally asked me about it, I was sure she would flip out. Not want to be my friend anymore. But when I explained that the mind reading was a borrowed power—a once-in-a-lifetime, never-to-happen-again strange thing—she vowed to keep it between us. And she did. She never told Miranda or

Avery or Tamara or any of the other girls at our lunch table, girls she'd known years before I showed up. She kept my secret because we were best friends.

Sometimes I wonder if I should've trusted her with the whole truth about me.

The whole truth is, I can do other things. Other supernatural things. Lots of other *supernatural* things. I can still read minds, too, if I wanted to, but I've learned how to block that power because believe me, it's way more trouble than it's worth. The other stuff I can't block. I'm not sure anymore that I'd even want to.

I think a lot about telling her, but I'm pretty positive that even she would be weirded out by what I can do. After all, my powers weird *me* out.

"Good morning, sleepyheads!" Mr. Randazzo boomed as we entered the kitchen. He stood at the stove. His wife's frilly floral apron tied haphazardly around his waist was a stark contrast to his torn jeans and Bruce Springsteen concert T-shirt. "A tall or short stack?"

"Tall, for sure!" Lily answered for both of us. Cammie was coloring at the large oak table, and her mother, already dressed for the day in a blue shirtdress, typed on a laptop next to her. The *thump* of a ball hitting a baseball glove floated through the open window. "The little beasts?" Lily asked.

"Yes, your three brothers are already outside causing chaos," her dad replied as he furiously whisked pancake batter in a white ceramic bowl.

"Sam! It's getting everywhere!" Mrs. Randazzo cried.

Mr. Randazzo glanced at the batter-splattered counter and shrugged. "That's what the sponge is for. You see, girls, the secret to great pancakes is the wrist motion. Quick flicks." He demonstrated and the batter erupted, dripping over the edge of the bowl onto the already dirty counter.

Lily's mom started to stand.

"No!" her dad cried. "Lily, make her stay put. It's her day, after all."

Lily's eyes grew wide with sudden realization. She leaped forward and wrapped her mother in a massive hug. "Happy Mother's Day to you!" she sang to the tune of "Happy Birthday." Lily loved holidays. She made a big deal out of even Groundhog Day and Arbor Day. Lily sang her song all the way through, and Cammie joined in.

I stood awkwardly by the table. Mrs. Randazzo wasn't my mother. I stayed silent and watched. I'd forgotten it was Mother's Day. It wasn't a holiday I ever circled on the calendar.

Lily gently guided her mom back into her chair. "Dad has it under control."

"So he says." She glanced dubiously at the batter dotting her husband's wavy black hair, then at the dishes stacked precariously in the sink. She fingered the sticky table where earlier the boys had dripped syrup. "Maybe I'll just—"

"Just relax," Mr. Randazzo ordered. "I've got this. It's *Mother's* Day. Lily and Sara, entertain her. Distract her. Anything. *Please*."

"Are you working on the fund-raiser?" Lily slid into the chair next to her mother and purposely blocked the view of Mr. Randazzo's backhanded pancake flip.

"I'm making a chart of all the donations." Mrs. Randazzo and Lily shared the same thick dark hair, olive skin, and high cheekbones. I often thought Lily looked like a mini version of her mom. Everyone says I look like my mom too, with our blond hair and light-blue eyes. Lily's mom turned to me as if noticing I was there for the first time. "Cammie, scoot down and make room for Sara."

"I should just go." I took a tentative step backward. I didn't want to leave, but it was Mother's Day, after all. I didn't belong here. "It's a family holiday and . . ."

"Oh, get over here, silly." Mrs. Randazzo patted the place next to her. "You are so a part of this family, Sara. Believe me, I need some more girl power to balance out the boy egos in this house."

"Ego? What ego?" Mr. Randazzo called. "I am only the best pancake maker in all of the Jersey shore."

"You are needed here, Sara. Badly," Lily's mom said, smiling widely at me.

If I couldn't be with my own mom this morning, Lily's mom was definitely next best. I squeezed a chair between her and Cammie. "Hey, Camsters. I like that you're coloring the tree purple. Trees should definitely be purple."

Cammie handed me a darker shade of violet from her enormous box of crayons, and I shaded in a pine tree. Cammie's full cheeks and broad forehead resembled her dad's, but she had the same magnetic sparkle in her eyes that made everyone at school hover about Lily, like moths attracted to light.

"Ohhh, is the shoe lady coming again?" Lily asked. She raised her voice to be heard over her dad's off-key singing. *"Born to run . . . baby, we were born to run . . ."* He was forever singing Springsteen songs.

"She is." Mrs. Randazzo tapped the screen. "She promised to bring twice as many as she did last year."

"Coming where?" I asked.

"Wow, that's right, you don't know about Bargain on the Boardwalk!" Lily exclaimed.

"Bargain on the Boardwalk is a fund-raiser for the local schools that happens every year. It's next weekend, in fact," Mrs. Randazzo explained. "It's a big Stellamar tradition—kind of the unofficial kickoff to summer for the locals before the tourists descend."

"It's the most amazing flea market, but not with junky stuff," Lily added. "Well, okay, there is some junky stuff that's donated, but there's also lots of really cool crafts and accessory vendors and people selling jewelry. Last year, this lady who works for some shoe company in New York brought all these amazing shoes. You know those cute aqua sandals

I have with the chunky heels that make me almost tall? I got those for only fifteen dollars. Fifteen! Don't they look like they cost a lot more?"

"They do," I agreed as Lily's dad set down a mountain of pancakes dripping with butter. I attempted a sincere smile as Mr. Randazzo sang, *"Hungry heart . . . ,"* but I was the only one. His Springsteen soundtrack had become background noise to his family.

"We have ten different jewelry vendors this year. This one guy, a new vendor this year, weaves together the thinnest silver wire into stunning necklaces. I know he's going to be a big hit." Mrs. Randazzo squinted at her list. "We need more stuff to be donated, though. We make the most money on the high-end rummage sale items. I do hope we get enough—"

"Don't worry about it today," Mr. Randazzo scolded. He plopped into a chair and sipped a mug of coffee, the mess by the stove and the promise of using a sponge temporarily forgotten. "Your mother needs to be stopped before she completely heads up Bargain on the Boardwalk again." She started to protest, and he gently cut her off. "It's a lot of work, honey. You can't do it all by yourself!"

"I'm going to help," Lily said, already finishing her second pancake.

"Me too," I offered. "What should I do?"

"See what you have to donate in your house. We'll take anything as long as it's clean and working," Mrs. Randazzo said.

"Sure." That sounded easy. "Hey, I bet Lady Azura has some really great stuff to donate."

"Seriously! Can you even imagine what she has? It's like opening some old-fashioned movie star's closet." Lily loved Lady Azura's style.

"Lady Azura does have classy clothes," Lily's mom said. "But for some reason, she's never given anything to the sale before."

"Really?" I was surprised. Lady Azura was quirky and more than a little odd, but she was one of the most generous people I'd ever met. "I'm sure she will if I ask her."

"I bet so too," Mrs. Randazzo agreed. "Especially today."

"Wow, yeah. I kind of forgot to . . . Should I make her a card or something?" I fumbled my words. I'd never had a great-grandmother before. I'd just found out this past Christmas that Lady Azura, the fortune-teller who lived and worked on the first floor of our house, was actually my great-grandmother. How did the Mother's Day thing work with great-grandmothers? I wondered. Was there some other special day for them or did you celebrate today?

"Lady Azura would love a card." Lily's mom glanced around her sticky, splattered kitchen. "Or take her out."

"Ahh, I'm wounded." Her husband clutched his chest playfully.

Lily snorted, then turned to me. "Let's go help sort the donations down at the community center."

"Not now," Mrs. Randazzo said. "We're expected at Aunt Angela's for Mother's Day lunch."

"Lunch?" Lily eyed the demolished stack of pancakes. "Can't I skip it?"

"No chance. Great-Aunt Ro and Aunt Dani's family are going to be there. And your cousin Lauren Grace." Lily had more relatives in our little town than Cammie had crayons in her big box. "Sara, you should come too," her mom offered.

"Thanks"—I pushed back my chair and cleared my

plate—"but I'm going to go home and make a card or present or something for Lady Azura."

At that moment, the back door at the far end of the kitchen slammed open, letting in a whirlwind of yelling and pounding feet. Sammy, Joey, and Jake pushed forward, all talking at once.

"What's happened?" Mr. Randazzo sounded alarmed as his sons noisily surrounded him.

The barking answered his question.

For a moment, everyone grew silent. A small dog with filthy matted fur scampered excitedly at the boys' heels. The dog panted and yapped insistently.

"Doggie!" Cammie exclaimed, setting everyone back into action.

Lily immediately fell to her knees and gathered the dirty creature in her arms. "Oh, you poor little thing."

"Lily," Mrs. Randazzo cautioned. "You have no idea where that dog came from, if it's vicious, if—"

"He's friendly, Mom," ten-year-old Sammy interrupted. "He ran up to us in the yard and started playing ball."

"Hold on a second." Mr. Randazzo knelt beside Lily. "Somebody must've lost this dog."

"There's a collar, but no tags," Lily pointed out, rubbing the dog behind its pointy ears. "Hi, sweetie," she cooed as the dog licked her hand, then licked her father's elbow. Sammy was right. He *was* friendly.

"That's odd." Mr. Randazzo inspected the dog. "No name or phone number anywhere. Other than being filthy, he doesn't look like a stray. He's well fed."

"That stinky dog needs a bath," Mrs. Randazzo declared, pulling Cammie away.

I eyed the dog cautiously. His walnut-brown fur was tangled with tiny burrs. His black eyes skittered from face to face, and his stub of a tail wagged furiously.

"Can we wash him?" Lily asked. "I'll do it outside with the hose." She hadn't stopped petting the dog. Lily loved dogs. She planned to have three when she grew up. She'd even picked out the names—Kiwi, Cupid, and Coco, I think. She was forever begging her parents for a dog, but her mother always put her off, saying, "Someday." I didn't need to read Lily's mind to know what she was thinking.

"Can we keep him?" Six-year-old Jake blurted the question Lily had been trying delicately to frame.

"No, honey, this is someone's dog. We need to call

the police and the shelter. Some sad person is missing him," his mom said gently.

"What if nobody claims him?" Lily asked. "Maybe he was abandoned."

All the kids chimed in, begging to keep the scruffy little dog.

Mrs. Randazzo sighed and shot her husband a look that said, *Back me up here.*

He ran a hand through his hair. "Here's the plan. Boys, get a towel and let some water sit in the tub in the sun for a bit to warm it up. Lily, go grab some shampoo and towels and supervise giving this dog a bath while I call around. We will find his owner and return him nice and clean."

"But what if there's no owner—"

Lily's dad cut her off. "We need to look. He's not our dog."

Lily nodded, but I could tell that she had already adopted him in her heart. The boys and Cammie ran outside. Mrs. Randazzo began to load the dishwasher, while Mr. Randazzo disappeared into the other room to make the phone calls.

"Sara, you have to pet him." Lily waved me over.

"Isn't he the sweetest? Look at his little black nose!"

I knelt beside Lily. The stench of dirty dog was overpowering, but I reached out my hand to rub his back. His body felt warm. "He is cute," I admitted. My fingers rested on the green woven collar around his neck, and suddenly I saw the children.

Not Lily's brothers or sister. These kids were blond, their straight hair even lighter than mine. A boy and a girl with similar features. Brother and sister. Maybe twins. They looked to be about six.

I inhaled the perfume of lilacs and freshly cut grass. Birds chirped from a nearby tree heavy with pink cherry blossoms. I stared in amazement as the boy and girl sprawled on a lush lawn, their bare toes poking out from their jeans, and hugged the dog.

The dog's green collar gleamed against its groomed brown fur. Clean. The dog was suddenly clean. I glanced around for Lily. Where was she? Who were these little kids? How did we get outside?

The kids giggled as the dog licked their faces. An older boy raced toward them, his white-blond hair cut into a spiky crew cut. I sucked in my breath.

He was really cute. As cute as Jayden, I think,

though he looked nothing at all like Jayden. He had the most incredible, piercing green eyes. Eyes that appeared mischievous and playful, and then, for the briefest flash, I saw the glimmer of something else. Something I recognized. This boy had secrets.

"Go fetch, Buddy!" the boy called as he tossed a red Frisbee across the lawn. The little dog sprinted and—

"Grab him, Sara!"

Lily's voice. I blinked, unable to move as the dog wriggled free and raced about the kitchen.

The batter-splattered kitchen.

Inside the Randazzos' house.

No blond twins on the grass. No cute boy with a Frisbee. Just Lily and her mother chasing the filthy stray dog across the tile floor.

What had just happened?

Chapter 2

What should have been a minute's walk home took the longest time. My brain flooded with questions.

I saw something with that dog. But what? Was it *dead*?

You see, that's my big secret. I can see spirits. Dead people. And I can do more than just see them. I can talk to them. Interact with them. Sometimes they won't leave me alone.

I've been seeing them since I was little. I haven't told Lily yet. The only people who know my secret are my dad and Lady Azura. Lady Azura and I share the same powers, though I'm still not sure all Lady Azura can do now that she's so old and her powers seem to be rusty. Seeing and talking to the dead seems to be a genetic trait in our family, the way Lily inherited her mom's hair and Cammie her dad's forehead.

Lucky me.

But that dog wasn't dead, I thought. It had to be alive if Lily and her brothers were petting it, right? I knew there were rare times when dead people's spirits could be seen by everyone—it had happened with this boy Kyle, who Lily had a big crush on because she didn't know he was really a spirit—but that was really rare, and I didn't think this was the case with the dog. The dog felt totally real to me. Alive. I was sure of it.

I kicked one of the yellow pebbles that line the driveways in our shore town. It skittered over the uneven sidewalk. The panicky feeling pushed against my lungs. This was the feeling I got when my brain couldn't keep up. When weird things happened too fast. It was different from the sick feeling I got when I connected with a spirit.

Mind reading, I decided. I must have read the dog's mind.

I shook my head and sent another pebble airborne. But that wasn't it either. I had learned how to block that ability. Lady Azura had taught me, and she knew what she was doing. Besides, I didn't feel like I'd tapped into the brain of a dog. No, it had played like a scene streaming on a video. I wasn't part of it, exactly, not like in a vision. I'd had those, too. But this had been something else.

What had I seen? My brain circled back to the same question.

I closed my eyes, trying to hit rewind. Had I imagined it? I didn't think so.

His face appeared. Spiky blond hair. A golden, even tan, as if he spent lots of time outdoors. Mystery Boy was definitely cute.

"I find walking a lot easier when I open my eyes."

I'd bumped into my dad on the sidewalk in front of our house.

"Were you and Lily up all night?" Dad chuckled when he noticed my PEACE, LOVE, DREAM shorts and matching tank. "Pajamas? Still?"

"I didn't get around to putting on real clothes. I'm tired," I admitted. *And confused,* I thought, but kept that to myself. Supernatural stuff put Dad on edge. Talking about it caused these little dots of sweat to spring up on his forehead. He thought he masked his unease, but I knew. Now that I had Lady Azura, I tried not to bother him with it. She'd answer my questions. "What are you doing, Daddy-o?"

"Prying up these cracked pavers, so I can lay a new walkway." He knelt and wedged a metal rod under one of the old gray stones. Part of our deal when we moved into the top two floors of Lady Azura's house was that Dad would help with repairs. The old Victorian had gotten really run-down.

I tossed my terry overnight bag on the grass and told him about Bargain on the Boardwalk. "Do you have anything to donate?"

He tipped the rim of the baseball cap resting on his sandy-brown curls. "Hmm . . . not that I can think of. I purged when I packed to come out here." We had arrived from California pretty slim on supplies. Dad really had wanted to start over.

"What about old tools? You have lots of those. I saw a pile in the shed out back."

"They're pretty beat up." He chipped at a stubborn piece of flagstone. "I'll grab some when I'm done, but don't expect them to be big sellers. You know, I did ship some boxes out here that I just dumped in the attic. Mostly old stuff. But you could look in there and see if there's any hidden treasure."

"Could I?" I snatched my bag and hopscotched over the remaining pavers. "That would be—"

"But . . . ," Dad called before I made it to the porch.

I stopped and faced him. "Always a but," I teased.

"That's right, kiddo. I was going to say, please run whatever you pull out by me, okay? There's some stuff in there with sentimental value, and I don't want some child across town dressing her doll in your first birthday outfit."

"Got it." I hurried up the wooden steps and pushed open the front door. I'd check the attic and then grab my camera, I decided. I had the best idea. I'd take a photo of the purple-and-gold-painted sign propped in the first-floor window that advertised Lady Azura's fortune-telling business, manipulate the colors on my computer, then do a repeat pattern of it like this famous artist Andy Warhol did with a soup can. It'd make the perfect card. Maybe even a poster—

"Oh, my dear! What happened to you?" Lady Azura raised one hand to her mouth; the other cradled a porcelain teacup with painted pink roses.

"Nothing. Why?"

"Wandering about town in your nightclothes, and your hair is . . . a sight." She wore an ivory shift dress. Several strands of colorful glass beads hung heavily around her slender, wrinkled neck. Lady Azura always dressed up. She wore silk gowns to bed. Mini marshmallows bobbed in the antique cup as she sipped hot chocolate and eyed me critically. "Something is different with you."

"I need a shower. Forgot to brush my teeth too," I admitted. "It was crazy at Lily's this morning. Oh . . . Happy Mother's Day!"

She paused, almost as if she didn't understand the words. Then a smile played across her crimson lips. I'd surprised her.

"Sara, you have made my day. Mother's Day. It's been a long time. . . ."

I debated singing Lily's Mother's Day song, but that's not really me. And it certainly wasn't Lady Azura. She didn't do silly, as far as I knew. Making her the present would be way better.

She took a step closer and touched my cheek. Her bony fingers were icy, even though they'd just been holding a steaming cup. "Something has shifted."

"Shifted?" I had no idea what she was getting at.

"Follow me." She pushed aside the thick, purple velvet curtains covering a doorway.

Entering her fortune-telling room was like tearing back the wrapping of the most wonderful present. The anticipation of all the possibilities created tingles in my body every time. She flicked on two of the lamps with the beaded, fringed shades, bathing the room in a warm glow. Easing into the big armchair with the nubby, mustard-colored fabric, Lady Azura interlaced her fingers and continued to regard me.

"What?" I asked.

She just stared in this way that she has. It's not so much that she's looking at you, it's like she's looking into you.

"Hey, Lily's mom is heading up this big rummage sale on the boardwalk," I said, trying to divert her focus. "Do you know about it?"

"I do." She'd lived in Stellamar her whole life. Over eighty years. Of course she knew.

"There's a change in your aura," she said. "Your energy has shifted."

"I feel fine."

"I've sensed the shift since your birthday. Thirteen. A pivotal year. The colors about you . . . they've been blending, mixing, changing."

"What color am I now?" Lady Azura saw colors around people. They had something to do with the energy waves emitted by your body. I didn't really get what they meant or why they changed, even though Lady Azura was always trying to explain it to me. I used to be a pale green.

"I'm seeing cobalt blue mixed with a brilliant gold."

"Is that good?"

"It is interesting. Not good or bad. Just interesting." She pressed her fingertips together. "Change is coming."

"What kind?" I didn't know whether she was talking about normal body stuff or something else.

She was silent for a long time. I didn't like it when she got into one of her trancelike states. She seemed so distant. Like she wasn't really here. "So I'm helping Mrs. Randazzo get donations. Do you have clothes or jewelry to donate?" I moved toward the glass shelves lined with crystals and gemstones, making it difficult for her to keep examining me.

"No."

"You don't have anything?" I found that hard to believe. She had drawers and closets filled with scarves, accessories, and handbags I never saw her wear.

"No, I do not have anything I want to donate."

"But it's for a good cause. My school and other ones. They use the money to buy supplies and do assemblies."

"The schools are important." She tilted her head, as if trying to see me from a different angle.

"So you'll donate some things then?"

"No. My possessions are just that. Mine."

"But you must have things you don't use anymore." I could hear the frustration tighten my voice, but really now, she could give *something*. "I can look through your stuff if you don't want to be bothered. I'll be really neat and—"

"As a rule, I do not allow my personal belongings to be taken by people I do not know."

"They're not being taken. They're being sold to raise money—"

"I quite understand how a rummage sale works, Sara." She sighed. "I will write a check you can bring to Mrs. Randazzo as a donation to the schools. I am very happy to give money, but I must keep all my belongings with me."

Was this an old-person thing or just a Lady Azura thing? I wasn't sure. I'd never thought she was one of those hoarder people, but she *did* have a lot of stuff.

"Energy isn't found only in people," she continued. "Energy has the ability to transfer. Objects absorb energy. My objects absorb my energy."

I pointed to the china cup now resting next to the crystal ball on the large round table. "So that cup is filled with hot chocolate *and* your energy."

"Exactly."

I couldn't help it. I started to laugh. I pictured a teeny-tiny old woman swimming in a lake of hot chocolate, weaving about marshmallow islands.

"Time is speeding up, and you have a lot to learn, Sara." She didn't look upset that I was laughing. Concern filled her eyes. A sort of motherly concern. "We need one of our lessons." Her tone had taken on a sudden urgency. "I have much to tell you."

For the last couple of months, she'd been teaching me about our powers. How they worked. How to control them. The rules, or what she knew of them. Lots of things were fuzzy, I'd discovered. It wasn't like there was a huge textbook with all the directions.

"Maybe later." I yawned and turned to go upstairs. "I'm not focused today, okay?" I was also kind of irritated with her. I'd promised Mrs. Randazzo I'd get her to donate. I hadn't thought it would be hard.

"Do not wait too long," she warned. "The shift has started."

The attic floorboards groaned. My bare feet left prints in the thin coating of grime collected over the hundred years this house had looked over the bay. Dust tickled my throat, and I wondered why I'd bothered with the shower and clean clothes.

I paused and glanced about nervously.

Even people without my powers know that ghosts hang out in attics. There were ghosts on all three floors of this house—the man with the sailor cap, the mustached businessman, the woman who wouldn't stop knitting, and the boy who lived in my crafts room closet. I didn't know who lurked here, since I made a point of rarely coming up. Why go looking for dead people? They found me easily enough.

I waited in the silence. I could often feel their presence before they materialized.

Nothing. I was alone.

My eyes wandered over to the corner where a tall trunk stood. Lonely. Waiting. Beckoning.

No, I told myself. *That's not why you're here.* I forced myself to look away.

I took a deep breath, coughed on more dust, and searched for Dad's boxes. The attic overflowed with Lady Azura's junk. Rolled-up Oriental carpets, ceramic lamps, an elaborate but tarnished full-length mirror, an assortment of suitcases in all shapes and colors. *Seriously?* I thought. *There's a ton up here she could donate.* She wouldn't know if I took anything, I realized. Lady Azura's arthritis prevented her from climbing the stairs beyond the first floor. I reached for a stack of lace place mats, then pulled back. She would be so angry if she found out.

I'll talk to her about it again, I decided. Maybe she was just in a bad mood.

I spotted several large cardboard boxes off to one side. SAVE—MIKE COLLINS was scribbled on each one in black Sharpie in my Dad's scrawl. I folded back the flaps of one and peered inside.

Plaster molds of my hand when I was in preschool. A chipped piggy bank that I didn't recognize, with my name painted on the side. Those would fall into the sentimental value category, I figured. But then I came across several fancy stuffed animals, all in good condition, that I remember getting as presents a few years ago from one of my dad's old girlfriends. I put them aside. No sentimental value there. They could be donated, and so could a marionette of a unicorn that I could never work without tangling the strings.

In the next box, I dug through old Halloween costumes, grinning when I pulled out my furry Dalmatian suit. Dad had dressed as a firefighter and I was the "fire dog." The rest of that year, first grade, I think, I'd come home from school and change into the outfit to watch TV. Dad thought I had a thing for "fire dogs." He bought me all these Dalmatian figurines and toys. It really was just that the costume was comfy, like a worn-in blanket.

Everything in the boxes cried out *Sara Collins and her dad*, I realized. Every object was traceable to some memory the two of us shared. Together. Me and Dad.

It's not just the two of us, though, I thought. *She's here too.*

My gaze shifted back to the vertical wardrobe trunk tucked under the dormer window. Slowly I made my way over. Shadows darkened, and goose bumps rose on my bare arms. I lay one palm on the trunk's surface. "I'm here," I whispered.

It'd been a long time.

My trembling fingers unclasped the line of brass fastenings. My heart thumped with excitement and nervousness. I pulled the handle, and the hinges cried in protest as the two sides parted. I caught the faintest whiff of her perfume.

I peered inside and whispered, "Happy Mother's Day, Mom."

Chapter 3

My mother wasn't in the trunk, I knew that. She died when I was born. Lady Azura had had a vision about it. She knew that my mom, her granddaughter, would die if she got pregnant, but no one believed her at first. When it did happen, my dad flipped out, scooped me up, and ran to California, away from his wife's spooky, supernatural grandmother. He never wanted to talk about my mom's death or return to New Jersey again.

Then I grew up. And starting seeing dead people. And here we are.

The trunk was filled with vinyl dress bags, all keeping my mom's favorite dresses safe. My dad had shared the trunk with me a few months ago when I'd needed a dress to wear to a dance. Besides photos, they're the closest thing I have to her. These dresses touched my mom's skin.

Most of the dresses in here were really fancy—I guess my parents used to go to a lot of parties. And most probably wouldn't fit me for at least a few more years, though I had been able to find one to wear to that dance with Jayden. When my dad saw me in it, he'd gotten all teary eyed and said I looked just like my mom.

I'd vowed to open the trunk only on special occasions. I didn't want the scent of her to evaporate. I danced my fingertips over the bags—seven hung on one side of the wardrobe, eight on the opposite side. I gingerly unzipped a navy bag and slipped out a magenta taffeta V-neck dress with a pouffy skirt. The thick fabric rustled under my touch. I held up the fancy dress, admiring the fitted bodice, then pressed it against my chest. Closing my eyes, I tried to imagine her wearing it.

Someone laughed. A high, lilting chortle.

My eyes snapped open. Still clutching the dress, I whirled about. "Dad?"

Silence. Dad wasn't up here. He was still outside, I

knew that. Besides, he didn't laugh like that. That was a female laugh.

"Lily?" Had she come by early? "Is that you, Lil?"

The attic seemed quieter than ever. I could hear my own rapid breaths.

Had I imagined it?

I gulped. *Don't freak yourself out,* I warned myself. I moved toward the large mirror, monitoring the shadowy corners and peering around the sheet-draped furniture. Listening for someone, making sure I was alone.

I gasped when I saw the dress reflected back at me. The deep pink made my eyes shimmer like blue topaz. *She must've looked so pretty,* I thought. Swaying, I moved the heavy skirt from side to side. The fabric produced a satisfying swish, and I imagined my mom dancing.

I hummed a popular song by a new Korean all-girls group that Lily loved, plastered the dress against my front, and danced. *Such a party dress!* I thought. I leaned into the rapid beat, shimmying my hips, singing the song.

Lyrics echoed in my head. *"I believe I can touch the sky . . . I think about it every night and day . . . Spread my wings and fly away . . ."*

Lyrics sung by a voice other than my own. Not the song I was singing. A different song sung by a man. A song I could hear around me.

I searched the attic for the source of the music. An iPod? Radio? Nothing.

The ballad played on. Suddenly in the mirror I spotted a retro CD player blasting the song. I twisted around, but the CD player wasn't behind me. Where was it? If I could see its reflection and I could hear it, I reasoned, it must be—

Then I spotted her.

She stood before me. In the mirror. *Through the mirror?* Wearing the magenta dress.

"Mom." My voice came out as a choked whisper.

She peered into the mirror, singing as she fastened a sparkly hoop earring. She didn't hear me or see me. So close. She was so close.

He moved up behind her and my legs trembled, nearly knocking me off balance. I didn't dare speak. My mother and my father. Together.

"You look so beautiful," he murmured into her ear. He was so young.

She smiled, and I flushed with the brilliance of her

35

joy. "I do, don't I? I'm going to dance all night! *I believe I can fly . . . ,*" she sang, then tilted her head toward him. "Need help?"

"I can dress myself," he protested as he struggled with the knot of his tie. He pursed his lips in concentration. A look I knew so well.

"By the time you master that, the bride and groom will be celebrating their fifth anniversary!" she teased, then turned to help him.

"What would I do without you, Natalie?" he asked as she deftly knotted the royal blue material around his neck.

She grabbed his hands and twirled. The magenta fabric swung about her as she laughed.

And then she was gone. I stared at a skinny girl with knobby knees and a messy ponytail. A girl clutching a party dress.

Me. Alone.

I pressed my nose against the cool glass. The mirror that had let me in now blocked me from her. *My mom.* I'd seen her.

She was so happy and so in love.

I rubbed the taffeta against my cheek, remembering

how it had hugged her skin and glowed against the faint spattering of beauty marks on her shoulders. It was as if one of the photos of her had come alive. For the first time, I'd heard her voice. It was higher than I would've thought.

I'd been hoping to glimpse my mother ever since I discovered I could see the dead. But she never came. Never.

Until now.

I gathered the dress in my arms, smoothing the wrinkled material, and wondered if it had caused her to appear. Rubbing my fingers along the seams, I tried desperately to bring her back. To hear her laughter again.

The attic stayed silent.

Maybe I used this dress up, I thought frantically. *I need another.* I pushed the magenta dress onto the hanger and back into the garment bag and reached for another.

A little black dress with a beaded neckline. I ran my hands along the fabric, willing her to return. I pushed the dress against my bare skin and murmured her name over and over.

"Sara?"

I jumped at the sound of my name.

"Sara? Are you up there?" I swallowed my disappointment. Dad was calling from the bottom of the attic stairs. "Sara? Lily's here."

"Coming!" I called. "I'll be right down." I quickly stored the black dress in its bag, then locked the trunk. I didn't want Lily to see my mom's dresses. Not now.

I debated telling Dad or Lady Azura what had happened. Mom appearing was huge. Lady Azura would totally get that. She'd want to talk about it, analyze it, dissect how and why it had happened.

And maybe she could help explain something else. Why hadn't that happened the first time I was up here in my mom's trunk? Was it because my dad had been with me? But I had worn one of her dresses to the dance and still she had not appeared. Was that magenta dress special? Or did it happen because it was Mother's Day?

I had a lot of questions, but I decided I wasn't going to ask them just yet. For now, I was just going to keep my glimpse of my mom to myself, like a secret little present.

Chapter 4

"My mom won't let him into my bed, so he just snuggled up and went to sleep below me last night on a big pillow on the floor," Lily told her audience. She held up her phone and scrolled through a series of photos. "He is so cute. Look."

The little brown dog looked much cleaner than I'd left him on Sunday. I could now see he had a patch of white fur, sort of in the shape of a bell, on his right side.

All the girls squeezed shoulder to shoulder at our lunch table oohed and aahed. Lily animatedly described the dog's surprise arrival and how they'd searched and searched for his owners. They called the animal shelter. They checked missing pets message boards. They even made flyers and posted them along

Beach Drive and the adjoining streets.

"No one has claimed him," Lily reported.

"That's good, right?" Avery Apolito asked, crinkling her freckled nose. "Will your parents let you keep him?"

"No. They say he has an owner, even though no one has shown." Lily sounded annoyed, but I wasn't sure at whom. The no-show owner? Her stubborn parents?

"Maybe the owner is looking in the wrong place," Miranda Rich offered. She was always the most logical of our group.

"I say he doesn't have an owner," Avery argued. Tiny and spunky, she never hesitated to butt heads with Miranda. "I say Lily should keep him. She's always wanted a dog."

"I want diamond stud earrings," Miranda countered. "That doesn't mean I'm getting them anytime soon."

"A stray dog is not like diamonds," Avery retorted. "Her parents don't have to pay anything. We didn't pay for my two Labs. We picked them up at the shelter."

"You should bring the dog to the shelter," Miranda told Lily. "It's the right thing."

"Don't think my dad didn't try," Lily grumbled.

"The shelter was completely full. They asked if we wouldn't mind keeping the dog until they emptied out a bit or they found the owners. They're searching too." She said this like it was a bad thing.

"That's great!" Tamara exclaimed. "If the owners don't come back, the dog will get so cozy at your house, he'll have to stay. Your family practically won't have a choice but to keep him."

"I know, right?" Lily nodded her head in agreement. "But try explaining that to my mom." She ripped into a bag of pita chips, and the force of her frustration scattered them across the table.

"I think the dog is a stray with no family. Don't you, Sara?" Avery asked. "Don't you think Lily should get to keep the dog?"

"Lily should——" I faltered, then busied myself removing the crusts from my peanut butter and jelly in the most studied and artistic way possible. Everyone turned to me.

"She should what?" Miranda asked.

"Well . . ." As soon as I spoke, it struck me with incredible clarity, even though I suspected I'd known it when I saw the blond kids on the grass. The dog *did* belong to someone. "It wouldn't be fair if someone did lose the dog."

Lily's face clouded over. "You're supposed to be on my side, best friend," she grumbled.

"I am," I assured her, and fumbled with the growing pile of crusts. Lily looked wounded, and I felt horrible. Who was I to crush her hope? I wondered. What did I know, really?

I knew Lily wanted the dog, and I knew no one had claimed him. I also knew that Lily would be the best dog owner ever. The kids and the boy—I knew nothing about them. Absolutely nothing. I didn't know whether they were out there somewhere. I didn't even know whether I'd purely imagined them.

"I didn't say for sure someone did lose the dog." I smiled encouragingly across the table to Lily. "I bet no one did. I bet it will all work out."

The little hairs on the back of my neck tingled as I spoke. My shoulders rose reflexively. I sensed eyes on me. Watching. Staring. Not any eyes. *His* eyes.

Slowly I turned and scanned the cafeteria. Could *he* be here?

All the seventh graders were in motion, dumping

trays of half-eaten ravioli, sharing study guides for an afternoon test, dodging the monitor, and adding to the overall chaos with laughter and chatter. No one looked at me. No one at all.

He wasn't anywhere.

"What are you doing?" Avery asked as I accidentally pushed against her.

"Just looking," I said vaguely. I turned back to my mutilated sandwich and crumpled the foil around it.

I'd been so sure he was here, staring at me with his piercing eyes. It didn't make sense. I didn't know him. So why did I feel Mystery Boy had been listening to me—and judging me?

I couldn't get him out of my mind. His sun-bleached hair. His eyes. I zoned out for the rest of the dog debate and mechanically followed my friends as they filed out of the cafeteria.

"Look!" Tamara said suddenly. "I mean, don't be obvious, but look! There's *that* guy!"

My heart fluttered as my gaze followed the direction Tamara had nodded toward. Was it him?

"Let's go over." Avery grabbed my hand and gave a tug toward a boy I now recognized from photographing the soccer team last fall for the *Wire*. Number 52, I recalled from the back of his red jersey. His name I couldn't remember. Some boy from eighth grade. Not my Mystery Boy.

"Get a grip," I scolded myself.

"What?" Avery dropped my hand and scrunched her nose.

I hadn't realized I'd said that out loud. "Nothing," I mumbled. *I'm just looking for my imaginary crush in the school cafeteria,* I thought. How totally lame.

I tugged at the necklace I always wore. I'd started doing that when I felt frazzled. Six little crystals were stacked together on the black cord, each one given to me by Lady Azura. Each one contained a different essence. I brushed my thumb over the glossy silver hematite. A secure sense of self was what it promised. I could use a little of that right now.

"Wait. What are we going to do when"—Tamara glanced at the boy, a blush creeping to her hairline—"we get there?"

"Sign up for his club, obviously," Miranda said.

"How do you know it's a club?" Lily asked. "I think it's a car wash or a fund-raiser of some kind."

Miranda rolled her eyes. "Does it matter? Whatever the boy's good works are, Tamara supports them, and we support Tamara. Come on, before Tamara chickens out again." She nudged Tamara forward, and the four of us followed.

"Hi, we're here to volunteer." Lily's voice had an easy, musical quality. She never seemed nervous or awkward talking to boys.

He pushed a sign-up sheet forward. "Cool. The meeting is on Thursday after school."

Miranda elbowed Tamara.

"What's it for?" The words tumbled out of Tamara's mouth in a jumble.

The boy gestured toward a homemade sign we'd all missed. COLLECT SPORTS EQUIPMENT FOR SOUTH SUDAN.

"Oh, wow! Africa. That's really good." Tamara's blush darkened to fire-engine red. "No, it's probably not good. I mean, that they need stuff there. It's good that you're doing something about it. Africa, I mean."

The boy arched his eyebrow at her. "So do you want to help?"

"Definitely." She wrote her name neatly on the paper. No chance he wouldn't be able to read it.

Lily, Avery, and Miranda all signed up too.

I didn't know anything about South Sudan, and I had no real interest in collecting sports equipment, even though I'm sure it was a worthy cause. That didn't matter. I'd learned quickly that friends here stuck together. We'd all go to the meeting for Tamara. I would sign up too.

"We need people to design flyers and make a website and—" The boy rattled off a list as I searched my binder. Two pencils with broken points. A dried-out felt tip.

"Can I borrow a—" Miranda handed me her blue ballpoint pen before I finished. "Thanks." My fingers curled around the pen, still warm from Miranda's palm, and I leaned forward to add my name to the list.

"Is that your best?" a man's gravelly voice asked. "I'm having trouble believing that you're really trying, because if you are, it's not good enough."

I raised my eyes in surprise. A tall man with a square jaw and hard eyes stood before me. He glared, arms crossed, rolled-up shirtsleeves revealing strong-looking forearms. Two red pens with a black swirly logo stuck out of his chest pocket.

"Are you listening to me?" he demanded.

I nodded, dumbstruck. Who was this? A teacher? Not one of mine.

"You need to do better! Much better. You need to put in the time to get your grades up."

Grades? What grades? I had all As and Bs in my classes. At least, I thought I did.

"Don't you have anything to say for yourself?" A large vein above his right eye throbbed. "An F in social studies! A C-minus in math!" He shook his head in disgust. "I'm embarrassed for you and for me. If you don't start doing significantly better in school, you lose privileges. No computer, no texting, no nothing. Got it?"

"No." My voice shook. I didn't get it. Why was this mean teacher yelling at me? How could those be my grades? I turned to my friends. "Who is he?" I pointed toward the man glaring at me.

"Shhh." Lily hustled me away from the table. "Way to be obvious. His name is Griffin Ellery. He plays soccer."

"Not him." I looked back over my shoulder. The man was gone. "Did you hear what that guy said?"

"I know, right? He's going to totally fake Tamara into doing his whole community service project. The way he was talking to her, he so knows she's into him."

The man hadn't been here, I realized with a jolt. No one had seen or heard him. No one but me. I was sure he wasn't a spirit. No shimmery form. No sick, vomity feeling or the kind of headache I got when the dead appeared.

I should've been happy. The guy was gone, and he wasn't a spirit. That was good, right?

But instead of feeling happy, I felt a chill wash over me. Now I was seeing strange people, and they were yelling at me about failing in school. I knew it couldn't be true. I knew I had an A in social studies. It had always been my best class, even back in California.

But what if it meant that it was about to start happening? Was I going to start failing my classes?

Chapter 5

It was my idea to see the dog.

We always reached Lily's house first on the walk home, but Wednesday afternoon I decided to go in and hang out, even though Lady Azura was expecting me. She'd want to send me to Elber's, but the trip to the corner store could wait. So could her questions. I didn't want to share. Not now. Not until I could make sense of the things I was seeing and feeling.

Lily hesitated on the step. "I don't know what I'll do if he's not here," she whispered.

"He's been here every day up until now," I offered.

"But what if today—" She broke off as the barking began. We could hear nails scratch against the hall floor as the dog scrambled to the other side of the door. He barked, then panted wildly as Lily hurried to fit her key into the lock. A minute later, she threw open the door and scooped the excited dog into her arms.

"He really loves you," I said, laughing as he slobbered over Lily's cheeks and then her arms.

Lily beamed. "I love him too. Isn't he the best?"

"Oh, Lily, he's drooling all over your new shirt!" Mrs. Randazzo exclaimed, entering the hall from the kitchen. "Pull that dog off you."

"I can't," Lily said. "We're attached. Him and me. Me and him."

Her mother shook her head. "You're not attached. You're dog-sitting until his owner comes back. Right, Lil?"

"But his owner hasn't come back," Lily stated matter-of-factly.

"He's not ours," Mrs. Randazzo said as she reached out to run her fingers through his silky coat. She was trying to be tough, but I could see she was falling for the dog too. At least a little. "The shelter called."

Lily's eyes filled with alarm. "Why?"

"They've had some adoptions this week. They think they will have room to take Dog here on Monday."

"But what if we don't want—"

Her mom cut her off. "Lily, please. We want what's

best for this dog, and what's best is to find his family. Flyers are up all over. I'm sure his owner will track us down." She tucked a stray piece of hair into her loose ponytail and softened her tone. "The boys are watching Cammie out back. Come out, girls. There's lemonade." She wove her way through the family room and out the sliding glass door.

"She won't even talk about it," Lily grumbled, setting the dog back on his four feet. "Can't she see he belongs with us?"

"If I were a dog, I'd want to live with your family," I said, trailing Lily and the dog to the back door.

"Right? We would be such an awesome dog family." Lily stepped onto the weathered gray deck. "It's actually cruel to this dog that he doesn't get to live with us."

"Stop with the melodrama, Lily," her mom called. She sat with Cammie on an oversize blue-striped towel. Cammie waved to me, then plucked periwinkle from her enormous box of crayons.

Lily pinched her lips together, trying not to talk back to her mom.

"Hi there, cutie," I said, squatting down to pet the

little dog. "You like it here, don't you?"

"I'm going to the kitchen to get Dog a treat," Lily announced.

"Get us a treat too!" Joey yelled from the grassy area below the deck. He twirled a lacrosse stick and sent the tiny ball soaring to Sammy.

I sat cross-legged next to Cammie and her mom. "Pick a color," Cammie offered, nudging the box toward me. What color would Lady Azura say I was today? Pale green? Cobalt blue? I was feeling sort of red-orange, whatever that means.

The little dog stepped onto the towel, made several circles, then plopped down, his back resting gently against my knee. "The dog wants to color too," I informed Cammie. "What color should we pick for him?" I scanned the rainbow of choices.

"Green like his collar," Cammie declared.

Plucking out the kelly-green crayon, I held it up against the woven fabric around his neck, pushing back curls of fur. My breath caught in my throat.

I stared, gaping at the boy's back. His pale spiky hair and the confidence in his shoulders told me it was him.

He was outside somewhere, facing a brick wall. "Why is this happening to me, Buddy?" he asked as he sank down to sit on the ground, his head in his hands. Dog nudged him with his nose as if to try and cheer him up.

He was so close. I wanted to reach out and soothe him. Tell him that I understood the loneliness that came with being different. That I knew exactly what he was feeling. I felt it too. His frustration flooded my veins and tensed my muscles. A buzzing sound invaded my brain.

But I couldn't touch him. I couldn't move. All I could do was watch. And feel.

Mystery Boy pulled the dog close, pressing him against his body. "Only you get it, Buddy. Only you listen to me." He buried his face into the dog's fur.

The buzzing stopped. And then I felt calmer. The boy looked up. His fingers lazily stroked the dog's back, his emotional whirlwind downgraded. By a dog.

His dog.

"Sara? Sara? Where'd you go?" Mrs. Randazzo's voice brought me back.

I stared blankly at the towel, then released my

death grip on the dog's collar. He'd fallen asleep in the sun.

Where *had* I gone? "Daydreaming, I guess," I admitted sheepishly.

"About a cute boy?"

How did she know? I narrowed my eyes, pondering what to say. I'd caught Lily's mom looking sideways at me before, especially when spirits moved about.

"You can tell me," she coaxed. "A boy in your grade? I used to daydream about Kevin Dowd. He was in the grade ahead of me. Gorgeous auburn hair. Never knew I existed. I put a spell on him."

"A spell?" My bulging eyes betrayed my shock.

She laughed, low and deep. "My friend Suzanne and I made a potion out of kitchen herbs and olive oil and sour cream and chanted a rhyme. It didn't change anything. What silly girls we were." She tousled Cammie's hair. "Mommy was silly."

"Dog!" Lily slid the door closed. "Here, Dog! Come, Dog!" She leaned forward.

The little dog opened one eye, then, disinterested, closed it.

"The dog needs a name," Sammy called. "He

doesn't know you're speaking to him."

"He has a name," Lily retorted. "Dog."

"How would you like it if I called you 'Girl'?" Sammy asked. "Girl, why didn't you get me a snack too?"

"Because you're not cute and cuddly," Lily retorted, then turned to her mom. "We really need to name Dog."

"Fluffy," Cammie offered. "No, Chocolate!"

"No way!" Sam cried. "I like Trevor or Freddie."

"Norton," Joey said. "That's the best name."

"I should be the one to choose," Lily announced.

Mrs. Randazzo shook her head. "This isn't a good idea. We shouldn't name a dog we do not own."

"Here, CocoLuxe! Come, CocoLuxe!" Lily tried, ignoring her mother. The dog ignored Lily.

"Hey, Ace!" Jake shouted. His two brothers and Cammie tried their names. The dog lay on the towel, unresponsive. Lily called him Chestnut, Bailey, and Juan Carlos. The dog still didn't care.

I bit my lip as they volleyed names about. *Wrong, wrong, wrong,* I thought. Finally I couldn't hold back. "Buddy. I think his name is Buddy."

"Yuck," Lily said. "That's a boring name. I like more exotic names. How about Carob?"

"Buddy," I insisted.

"Carob! Carob, cutie, come here!" Lily called from across the deck. The dog gazed at her but stayed still.

"Try Buddy. Try it."

"Okay. Buddy! Here, Buddy." The little dog's ears twitched, and he tilted his head. Lily laughed as he raced into her open arms. "Buddy!" she repeated. "Your name is Buddy."

"He knows his name!" Sammy and his brothers gathered around the dog, all taking turns calling him Buddy.

"It's like Sara read the dog's mind," Mrs. Randazzo said, clearly amazed.

Lily stopped scratching Buddy's belly and gave me a long, hard look. She raised her eyebrows, questioning me.

I shook my head vehemently. "I *can't* read minds," I said. "Just a really lucky guess. That's all."

It wasn't, though.

"If Buddy has a name," Mrs. Randazzo pointed out, "then Buddy has an owner somewhere."

"No, Mom, it doesn't mean that." Lily's voice was desperate.

"Yes, it does," I agreed. I hated turning on my best friend, but it was true.

"Then where are they?" Lily demanded, stepping toward me. She folded her arms defiantly across her chest.

I thought about the times I'd seen Buddy. With the blond twins on the grass. Comforting Mystery Boy by a brick wall. I searched my brain for details. Landmarks. Anything about the places that I'd seen. I came up blank.

"I don't know," I admitted.

"See, nobody does. All Buddy has is us."

"For now," Lily's mom interjected. "Only for now."

Lily heaved a disappointed sigh and followed me to the front sidewalk as I headed home. I'd become obsessive about studying since my encounter with that man who'd told me I was failing social studies. "I have to keep Buddy, Sara. I just have to. He's the dog I always dreamed of having."

"I thought you always wanted a golden retriever, not a mutt."

"Buddy is perfect. Better than perfect." She twirled a piece of hair around her index finger. "Look, I get it that he's probably someone's dog. If that person comes back for him, well, I'll be sad but okay. But Sara, I cannot let Buddy go to the shelter on Monday and be put in a cage. Buddy needs a family."

I closed my eyes and saw the boy's green eyes dart as he tossed the Frisbee. Then the same eyes clouded with anguish as he hugged his dog for comfort. His connection with his dog made me like him even more. My heart fluttered faster thinking about him.

"I only have four days to convince my mom. You need to help me. Maybe together we can convince her. Please, Sara, I'm going to come up with a plan." Lily reached for my hand.

Even though I knew Buddy had an owner who surely missed him, what choice did I have? Best friends always come before boys in visions. At least, I thought so.

"I'll do whatever you want," I promised. "I'll help you keep Buddy."

Chapter 6

What's she doing in there? I wondered. I tapped the linoleum table with my pencil, keeping rhythm with the second hand on the clock. Her hour had been up ten minutes ago. Lady Azura usually didn't give clients extra time.

I tried to refocus on my social studies homework. Longest river in South America . . . highest mountain in South America . . . Mrs. Grasing had a standing appointment every other Wednesday night. She always appeared at the door in a black raincoat, no matter the weather, and never spoke to me.

Finally I heard the front door close and the *click-clack* of Lady Azura's gold kitten heels as she entered the kitchen and made her way to the pantry. "More, more. She's always looking for more."

"Do you keeping telling her stuff? Do new readings?" I didn't know what went on behind the velvet curtain. Lady Azura was a big believer in her clients' privacy.

"Sometimes you have to say the same thing many different ways before it can be heard." She found a packet of instant hot chocolate and poured it into a mug, then set the teakettle on the stove to boil. "Where is your father?"

"Upstairs." I filled in another answer on my South America worksheet as Lady Azura pulled out the chair next to me and sat. I did my homework upstairs with Dad when he was home. Setting up camp in the kitchen meant I wanted to talk.

"I missed you after school." She reached for my hands, causing my pencil to drop. Her cold, thin fingers entwined with mine, and she was silent, absorbing my energy. This used to freak me out until I realized it was kind of like a doctor taking a patient's temperature. "You're in turmoil," she diagnosed correctly.

I told her all about Lily and Buddy and the Mystery Boy. I left out how I thought he was so cute. How I was kind of crushing on him. Some things you don't share with your great-grandmother.

"Is helping Lily to keep Buddy wrong?" I asked.

"This boy and the children you've seen, when do you see them?" she asked, not answering my question. "Are you with the dog when it happens?"

"Yes. Should I tell Lily that I had a vision of the kids he belongs to? I feel like I'm lying. I think she deserves to know, even though it will make her really sad."

"Let's say you tell Lily and let's say she believes you, then what? How do you propose to find these children?"

"I don't know," I admitted. "Is there any way to . . . call them up?"

"These children? They're alive?"

I hesitated. Could I be seeing into the past? Could they be dead? "I'm pretty sure they're alive, because the dog was with them."

"Then you're in luck. When I call up living people"—Lady Azura stretched her thin lips into a smile—"I use the telephone."

"Don't joke about this! I feel responsible for Buddy."

"Don't." Lady Azura stood and moved toward the whistling kettle. "This dog is not your responsibility."

She poured the boiling water into the mug. "Is the dog well taken care of with Lily's family? Is he getting food, shelter, and love?"

"Yes. Definitely."

"And you said the Randazzos have posted notices and are working with the shelter to find the owners." She opened a plastic bag and sprinkled mini marshmallows on top of her drink. She had a thing for marshmallows. All candy, really. "What more do you propose to do?"

I shrugged. I hated keeping secrets. I could feel the weight of them in my stomach. I carried too many secrets around already. A perpetual stomachache I'd learned to live with.

She turned to me. "I am a firm believer in fate. Things happen for a reason, although it may not be the reason we assume or what we initially think is right and fair. For now, the dog is meant to be with Lily. Since you have no way to make the situation better, you should leave it alone."

"Then why am I seeing him? The blond boy? Why is he coming to me?"

"I have my suspicions." She sipped the hot

chocolate. Her crimson lipstick left an imprint on the rim.

"Well, what are they?"

"It is too early to discuss it. As I've said, things are shifting. Time will tell." She squinted at me, as if trying to see the unseeable. "I suspect that time is not far off. Wait here."

I stared blindly at my worksheet after she left the room. I felt there was something more to my seeing Mystery Boy. Something bigger than the dog. I just couldn't imagine what.

Lady Azura returned and set a small, clear gem on the table. "This is a Herkimer diamond. Add it to your chain."

"Wow! A diamond?"

"It's called a diamond because it shares the same double pyramid shape. It's actually an extremely clear quartz crystal. Its clarity is what gives it power."

"What power?" I asked warily. Lady Azura didn't just hand out crystals. They weren't jewelry to her. Whenever she gave me one, she'd sensed something was going to happen and that I needed extra help.

"The Herkimer diamond has the ability to fine-tune

emerging powers. You are entering a different phase. Now that you are older, you need more powerful gemstones."

"For what? What powers? What does this have to do with the boy and Lily's dog?"

"String the crystal on your necklace and wear it this week. Let's see what happens."

"You're doing that thing again," I complained. "Not telling me stuff about what's going on with *me*."

"Sometimes it is best to let life unfold. Experience it first and then ask questions later. There's no need to get ahead of yourself. Wear the crystal this week. I suspect next week we will have much to discuss." She reached for her hot chocolate. "That dancing show that I like is on TV, so I am off to my room. Good night."

I knew there was no use questioning her now. She wouldn't cave like my dad sometimes did. I'd have to wait. I had no idea what was coming and what the crystal would bring. If I had, I might not have been so quick to add it to my necklace.

WHERE R U??????

COMING, I texted Lily on Saturday morning.

She'd been helping her mom set up Bargain on the Boardwalk since dawn. By the time I'd passed through the arched STELLAMAR BOARDWALK sign leading off Beach Drive and gotten the okay from Lily's great-aunt Ro, who ran the information desk, to bypass the line and enter the sale early, rows and rows of folding tables piled high with everything from toaster ovens to beach cover-ups to gardening tools lined almost the entire stretch of the boardwalk. Men and woman adjusted displays, scribbled price tags, and straightened hangers, scrambling before the nine thirty opening.

I slowed at a collection of musical jewelry boxes, all lilting the same waltzing melody. Lady Azura owned something like this. Hers had hummingbirds painted on the top. I hadn't been able to get her to donate anything, no matter how many ways I'd asked. I reached out to wind one when my phone buzzed again.

WE NEED 2 TALK!!!!!! MEET ME @ SCOOPS.

Lily had been texting me all morning. I turned and hurried along the gray-weathered boardwalk toward her uncle's ice-cream parlor. She waited outside in shorts, even though the air still held on to the final whispers of spring coolness.

"It's Buddy," she said.

I shooed away two seagulls pecking doughnut crumbs and pulled her onto a nearby wooden bench. "What happened? Did the kids come for Buddy?"

"What kids?"

"His owners," I fumbled. "I mean, I just always thought they'd be kids." Lame save, I knew, but luckily, Lily was too keyed up to notice.

"No, no one's showed up yet. It's been almost a week. If someone was looking, they would've found him by now, right?" Her knees bounced as she talked.

I nodded, although I wasn't so sure.

"So I need to show my mom and dad how incredibly helpful it would be to have a dog. Almost like how Buddy would take care of us."

"How would that work? It's not like a dog can make dinner or drive to the market," I joked.

"Not that way. I'm going to teach Buddy how to fetch the newspaper and pick up little toys that Cammie leaves all over." Even behind her oversize sunglasses, I could see the excitement in Lily's eyes. "I downloaded articles about how to do it."

"That could work," I agreed. "The woman in the

wheelchair who runs the souvenir shop near the Salty Crab has a therapy dog that helps her do stuff like that."

"I know! I was thinking about her too." Lily frowned. "It takes a lot of work to train a dog. You've got to repeat and repeat and repeat until he gets it. You'll help me?"

"Sure. Tomorrow?"

"Excellent!" Lily wrapped her arms around me. "You're the best! Now, let's shop."

"You don't need any training for that," I teased.

"Some things come naturally." She jangled the stack of bangles on her arms. Lily had a weakness for bracelets. For sunglasses, earrings, and shoes, too.

I held up my purple patent wristlet bag. "I brought my leftover birthday money. Let's hit that table." I pointed toward a young woman in a high ponytail and a white-and-green geometric shift dress, who stood in front a display of chandelier and hoop earrings. Intricate silver rings were lined up on a large velvet tray.

"A lot of the jewelry is vintage," the woman said as we approached.

"Is it yours?" I asked.

She laughed. "I'm too young to have all this old jewelry. I collect it from estate sales, garage sales, and even pawnshops. Some of it I have to fix or add to, but this is all quality."

"These look like a spider wove them." Lily held gold filigree earrings alongside her face.

I glanced at the little white tag. "Those earrings are crazy expensive."

"Quality costs money," the woman said. "The jewelry on the other side of the table is less."

"This ring isn't that much." Lily plucked a chunky silver ring that resembled a belt buckle from the tray and dropped it into my palm.

"It's going to be too big for my finger." I slipped it on anyway. The silver felt surprising warm. Probably from sitting in the sun, I figured. I twisted the band . . . and she appeared.

Brown hair parted severely to the side, revealing a line of neglected gray roots. Bloodshot eyes staring at the three playing cards placed before her. A jack of diamonds, a two of hearts, and a four of diamonds. Her nails were bitten down, and in some places I saw little scabs where they'd bled. And on her finger, the ring. The silver belt-buckle ring. The ring that was on my finger too.

She twirled the band, agitated, as her gaze flitted between the cards and a pile of red plastic chips on the felt-lined table. A single chip lay apart from the others.

"Miss?" A man's voice. "What do you want to do?"

My mouth went dry. I, too, stared at the cards. What did I want to do? I didn't know. Why didn't I know? I had to make a choice.

"Hit me." Her voice wavered.

A card was placed next to her three. A nine of clubs. Was that good? I didn't know.

"Twenty-five," the man announced without emotion. "You needed twenty-one for blackjack. You went over. The house wins." His hand scooped away the pile of chips.

My throat constricted, and panic seized my lungs. I couldn't breathe. She'd lost. There was only one chip left. Only one. After that, there was nothing. Nothing at all.

"I bet one." She pushed the solitary chip forward with a shaky hand.

Oh no! This was it. No money in the bank. Rent past due. *Please, please,* I chanted silently, as I twisted the ring. Around . . . around . . .

I pulled the ring off.

She was gone. I stood next to Lily at the jewelry table. The ponytail woman's attention was on Lily and the hoop earrings she was looking at. I quickly dropped the ring onto the tray, as if it were toxic.

I reached for a necklace of oversize blue-and-purple enamel beads. Way too gaudy to really consider buying, but I wanted to erase the feeling of horrible desperation the ring had brought me. I fastened the necklace around my neck. My breathing returned to normal. I closed my eyes and inhaled the familiar salty air rising off the ocean.

My nose twitched as the sharp odor of peroxide and cloying fruit overtook the sea air. A blast of hot air hit my cheek.

I opened my eyes to find myself in a hair salon.

A pretty, red-haired woman with freckled skin expertly wielded scissors, cutting the wet hair of another woman who sat in a chair facing a mirror. The hairdresser wore a paisley skirt and chunky cork platforms, and as I watched her reflection, I noticed the necklace resting on her blue shirt.

A duplicate of the beaded necklace I now wore.

"So I was telling Lucia that I knew he liked me. Why else would he also stop by Eddie's to get coffee the same time I always do?" The hairdresser angled the hair around her client's long face as she chattered excitedly.

"Then what?"

The hairdresser tried to suppress her smile, but it was too big. "He asked me out!" She beamed. "He was really awkward about it. Totally nervous. So cute, right?"

The client tried to nod, but the hairdresser steadied her head with her hand.

"We went to that new taco place on Route 22. Neither of us stopped talking. We were finishing each other's thoughts. He's the one. I tell you, he's the one." Her joy bubbled inside her.

Inside me.

I felt lighter, as if my feet were no longer on the ground. A warmth spread throughout my body. The sun was hugging me.

"What's with that silly smile, Sar? I hate to tell you, but that necklace is way ugly." Lily's voice, near but far.

I watched the hairdresser, swaying happily as she reached for a hair dryer. I swayed too. Then hands wrapped around my neck.

"What?" I cried, and whirled about.

Lily stood behind me, holding the necklace. "This had to come off. Bad fashion choice."

I licked my lips and blinked rapidly, taking in the boardwalk, the sale, the seagulls. The hair salon was gone. That incredible feeling of elation, also gone.

"I—I don't like this jewelry." I tried to control the tremble in my voice. "Let's go somewhere else."

"For sure," Lily said, dropping the necklace on the table. "I think I see the shoe woman down there."

She reached for my hand, and I let her guide me through the thickening crowd. I glanced back at the woman with the ponytail, now handing a ring to teen-age girl. Why had I seen and felt all that? Was it her? Was it her jewelry?

Or was it *me*?

Chapter 7

At the next booth, Lily begged me to try on these cool gladiator-style red leather sandals, but I was scared. Scared of sandals! How crazy is that? Lily kept saying over and over again that I'd kick myself later if I didn't at least try them.

"Where else can you find shoes that cute for so cheap?" Lily challenged me. And I knew she was right.

My hands shook as I released them from the tissue paper nest in their box and slipped them on. I fastened the two buckles by my ankles, afraid to look up, afraid to see. I raised my eyes and . . .

They fit.

I stood in red sandals on the Stellamar boardwalk with hundreds of people now swirling about, and nothing changed. No one appeared.

"They look so good on you!" Lily crowed with a big grin. "You're buying them, right?" She held two boxes of shoes in her arms.

I nodded, more confused than ever.

By eleven thirty, when we met Miranda, Avery, and Tamara at John's Pizza, Lily had two pairs of sandals, a necklace, an airbrushed T-shirt, a hot-pink wallet, and nothing left to go in it. "I'm out of money already," she moaned.

I'd bought only the red sandals. I couldn't focus on all the bargains. I kept worrying about the woman at the casino. Did she win that last hand of blackjack? Why had she gambled away her life savings? Even though she didn't say that, I knew it, the same way I knew the ocean was salty.

Everyone took turns showing their treasures. I exclaimed over the woven leather headbands Tamara had bought. She said the woman made them all herself, and each one was different. I twirled one of the headbands in my hands, inspecting how she did it. Maybe I could make one at home.

"I got these dangly earrings," Miranda announced. "They're vintage." She passed them to me, and I nudged the box along the table with my elbow to Lily. Had they come from that woman's stand? I wouldn't risk touching them.

Instead I eyed the T-shirt she was wearing. Blue with a swirly black logo I recognized from somewhere. Was it a store in the mall? Lily was so much better at knowing brands.

"Guess who we saw?" Tamara's lopsided grin gave away the answer.

"Griffin!" Lily squealed. "What happened?"

"Miranda made me ask about helping him with his charity thing. It was kind of weird because he was with his friends, but she totally forced me."

"And?" I asked.

"And I said we would make flyers this weekend, and he's going to meet me before school on Monday to hang them in the halls."

"We?" Lily asked. "You know I can barely draw a stick figure."

"Please?" Tamara begged. "Miranda, can we all go to your house and do it on your new computer together?"

"I'll help, but not at my house. My computer's not good."

"Did you break it? My cousin C.J. fixes computers now. He'd look at it," Lily offered.

"No, it works." Miranda squirmed in her seat. "Actually . . . my parents are punishing me. They took it away."

"What'd you do?" Avery asked.

"Nothing." She brushed off the question. "They're just mean, and my dad's really strict, that's all."

"Ooh, must've been bad!" Lily propped her chin in her hands. "Spill it."

Miranda wouldn't meet Lily's eyes. "I didn't do anything bad, and it's so not a big deal. My dad just overreacts to everything." She pulled out her phone as if she needed to read a text. I knew she didn't. She was embarrassed, and I was embarrassed too, because suddenly I knew why her computer had been taken away.

It came to me in a rush. The logo on Miranda's blue shirt was the same as the logo on the window of Rich's Hardware in town—the store Miranda's parents owned. It was also the same as the logo on the red pens the man had in his pocket. The man I saw yelling about bad grades.

I'd thought he was yelling at me, but I'd been wrong. He was yelling at Miranda. He was Miranda's dad.

How badly was Miranda doing in school? I wondered. I wanted to help, but how could I? How could I explain how I knew about something so personal, about her dad yelling at her and calling her a failure? I still couldn't explain it to myself.

"We can use my computer," I offered. "Maybe, if it's okay, we could also study social studies together at the same time. Review for the test? I'm kind of having a hard time with the map identification section."

"That's great!" Tamara exclaimed. "I'm awesome on the South America stuff. I can help you."

Lily frowned. She knew I had an A in social studies. We'd done the map ID worksheet together the other day, and I'd gotten all the answers right. "But Sar—"

"I'd be into that," Miranda said. "I'm not so great on the map ID, either."

"It would be fun to do it together." I ignored Lily eyeing me and smiled at Miranda. I felt guilty, even though I hadn't done anything wrong. A study group would help her. Miranda was my friend, and I really wanted to help.

Lily started to say something, but I cut her off. "Tamara and Griffin will make a cute couple, don't you think?" I asked.

"Totally," Miranda agreed, eager to change the subject as well.

Tamara and Avery took the bait, and the conversation turned to boys. Lily joined in too, though I knew she'd probably ask me about my lie later. I'd have come up with a story about how Miranda had confided in only me. My stomach churned at the thought of lying to her.

"And speaking of cute boys . . . ," Avery was saying. She waggled her eyebrows at me and I realized she must have been talking to me. "So, who are you going to like now that Jayden is gone?"

Mystery Boy popped into my head, and I felt my cheeks turn red. Avery must have seen my expression and thought she had upset me by mentioning Jayden. "I'm sorry, Sara!" she said quickly. "We don't have to talk about it. I'm sure you'll find some cute new guy to crush on soon!"

My face must have turned even redder.

"Let's do another lap," Lily said, jumping in to

change the subject. "My mom said they're putting new stuff out at noon." In the history of the world, did anyone have a better best friend? I wondered.

Lily took the lead. We all followed as she expertly weaved her way through the crowds, targeting the tables with the best stuff.

"Look who's over here fishing for a bargain!" Avery called.

The two Jacks from our grade stood in front of a table piled with fishing poles, watching Luke pretend to fly-fish.

"You need to scale back on the jokes, Avery," the taller Jack taunted. "Clam up, in fact."

"Ha-ha, Jack. You need kelp. Remember you're not the only fish in the sea," she replied, raising her hand to high-five me. Heat prickled my neck. I swiped my hair off my sweaty skin as I watched their war of words. For the past month, Avery and tall Jack had been trying to out-pun each other.

"Crabby, aren't you?" Jack retorted.

"When you give up, let minnow." Avery grinned, showing off the blue rubber bands on her braces.

They volleyed puns back and forth. The boardwalk

seemed to move. Up and down. My stomach heaved as I fought to retain my balance. Up and down. I reached for the edge of the plastic folding table to steady myself.

Then I looked around.

A woman. I hadn't seen her approach. Gray hair, droopy eyes, a heavy sweater, and translucent. Her body shimmered as she hovered by a table next to the fishing gear. The table displayed a bunch of old-looking vases. A bored-looking man attended the table.

"Look at my beautiful vases. Come hold my beautiful vases," she beckoned in a voice barely above a whisper.

I gave a quick shake of my head. No. No way. The woman was dead. I wasn't engaging with spirits. Not here. Not now.

"Every Thursday, Simon bought me flowers. Dahlias. Every Thursday, I put my flowers in a vase. This vase for yellow dahlias, this one for pink, and this one for white. My vases must reside with someone who appreciates beauty. You appreciate beauty, don't you, young lady?"

Maybe I did, but I didn't want one of her vases.

I turned my back on her, but it wasn't easy. Her energy tugged at me, willing me to the table, pulling me toward her vases. I swayed unsteadily.

Block her out, I told myself. *Create a bubble.*

Lady Azura had taught me to wall myself inside my own good thoughts to keep malevolent spirits away. I didn't know whether she was malevolent. She was probably just trying to sell her wares the way the living vendors did.

I thought of my friendship with Lily. I thought of little Buddy wagging his stub of a tail. I fixated on the yummy peach frozen yogurt from the new place on Beach Drive. Happy thoughts. The woman glided away from me.

I watched as she slid behind a mother holding a little boy's hand. Silently, she guided the woman's free hand to a short round vase. She pressed the young mother's palm to the tinted glass, creating a connection between the woman, the vase, and herself. The spirit's lips curled into a smile, and immediately the woman smiled too.

"I like this vase, don't you, Simon?" she asked the little boy.

His name was Simon. How weird.

Young Simon nodded, but his attention was on

Luke and the two Jacks playing with the fishing poles.

"I wasn't planning on buying anything today," the mother murmured to the man at the table. He had pocketed her money and was now wrapping the vase in newspaper.

I followed behind Lily, Avery, Tamara, and Miranda in a daze as they moved down the boardwalk. How many times did people think they were making an independent decision, I wondered, when their choice was really guided by unseen spirits?

Now that I started really looking, I saw spirits everywhere. Crowds brought them out. A teen boy in old-fashioned bathing trunks dripped puddles of seawater as he shivered and stared toward the ocean. A muscular man in overalls nudged men in the crowd toward a table filled with rusty license plates. A shimmery woman, whose upper body was all I could make out, blocked the path of anyone heading toward a table of antique serving dishes.

I did the opposite. I pushed the dead away.

Me in, them out. Me in, them out, I chanted to myself, focusing on my barrier.

I'm getting good at this, I thought. For years spirits

had tortured me, and I hadn't been able to fight back. I was proud that I could keep them away all by myself.

Myself. I was by myself.

I hurriedly scanned the faces around me. Crowds pressed in from all sides. Where were my friends? I'd lost them in my chanting daze.

"Lily!" I called. My voice drifted into the roar of haggling voices. "Where'd you go?" I edged my way to the metal railing separating the boardwalk from the sand.

"You must find it."

An older woman loomed over me. She stood almost six feet tall.

"Excuse me?" I asked.

"Find the key," she implored. Her dark eyes, framed by rectangular black glasses, revealed anguish. Wrinkled skin hung off her angular cheekbones, and her silver-gray hair was styled in a pixie cut. A string of pearls peeked out of a striped button-down shirt. My eyes rested at the ends of her sleeves. Where her hands should've been. I couldn't see her hands.

"The key," she repeated. She had no hands. None at all.

She was dead too. Another spirit.

I darted around her, anxious to find my friends. I didn't know what she was talking about, and I didn't care. I hurried past Scoops and the Haunted Mansion. What was Lily wearing? Purple, I remembered. A purple shirt. Miranda had on olive green. I searched for them. Avery and Tamara were too short to stand out in the crowd.

Shoulders bumped me, and I could smell pungent peppers-and-onions breath. I stood on my tiptoes, searching and searching.

Then I saw the dog.

He looked exactly like Buddy.

He stared straight at me as if he had something to say.

Chapter 8

I no longer noticed people elbowing me as they pushed toward a table.

All I could see was the dog.

Everything receded as I moved toward him. Our eyes stayed locked as I stepped closer and closer.

He did look exactly like Buddy. I reached out to him. My fingers curled around his cast-iron body, and I lifted him off the table. He fit snugly in my cupped palm. I inspected the small figurine.

It was amazing. The metal figure was painted the same walnut shade of brown as Buddy's fur. I ran my fingers over a few nicks in the paint where the metal shone through. The dog had the same pointy ears and stubby tail. Even stranger, the white splotch painted on his side kind of looked like a bell, too.

I have to show Lily, I thought immediately.

I turned the metal dog over, noting how old and intricately crafted he appeared. He was heavy, too. I wondered where he came from.

"Do you want to buy it?"

A bald man stood behind the table. He wiped his shiny face with a black bandanna.

I'll buy him for Lily, I decided. It wasn't her birthday or anything. It would just be a best friend present. "How much?"

He scratched his head. "I'm filling in for a friend. Bathroom break." He turned over a few other figurines on the table—a cow, a horse, and a peacock—looking for prices, then shrugged. "How does five dollars sound?"

"Sounds good." I was glad I still had money left. I fished around in my wristlet. "Where is this from? It's really heavy for something so tiny."

"Beats me. My friend's always picking up junk from garage sales." He reached for my five. "Not that that's junk or anything," he hastened to add.

I froze for a moment, tightly clutching the bill. The ponytailed woman's jewelry had come from garage sales, and it made me see strange people and feel what they were feeling. Would this metal dog figurine do that too?

I focused on the weight of it in my palm and felt nothing else. Good. I was still solidly grounded here in Stellamar. I gave the man my money and tucked the little "Buddy dog" next to the shoe box in my brown-paper shopping bag.

My phone was in my wristlet. Glancing at the screen, I saw I had three texts from Lily, one from Miranda, two from Avery, and one from my dad. They were all looking for me.

Five minutes later I met up with my friends by the visitors' information desk. They were spreading all their jewelry, sandals, and picture frames across the welcome desk for Lily's great-aunt Ro to see. I left Little Buddy in my bag. I'd give him to Lily later, when everyone else was gone.

"Totally love this!" Great-Aunt Ro exclaimed. Several people wandered in to look at brochures, bus timetables, and the old photos on the walls. Great-Aunt Ro ignored them.

I pressed my back against a bulletin board, listening to Avery's play-by-play of how she'd bartered for a hair clip, when I felt a presence next to me.

Bile rose in my throat, and I pushed it down.

The tall woman. The spirit with no hands.

"The key opens forty-three," she said.

I stared at her flapping cuffs. Spirits' bodies often lost their form, making parts difficult to see.

She leaned close. The smell of mothballs made my head spin. "Forty-three," she repeated.

The sour taste moved its way back up my throat, threatening to take the pizza in my stomach along with it.

"I need to meet my dad," I managed to say. It wasn't a lie. He did want me to meet him at John's Pizza, of all places.

"Tomorrow, right?" Lily asked. "Buddy?"

"I remember," I said. The woman leaned down even farther. Her pearls dangled dangerously close to my face. I had to get away. I forced a wave, then bolted for the door. Once outside, I ran all the way to the pizza place.

The footsteps woke me.

Heavy, thudding steps. Down the hall. Moving toward me.

"Dad?" I whispered. "Dad?"

Even in the darkness, I knew it wasn't him. Dad was athletic, slim, and light on his feet. He never walked like that, especially not in the middle of the night.

I clutched my comforter. Darkness blanketed my bedroom, and for once, the old house was silent. The digital clock on my night table glowed faintly. 2:36 a.m.

The footsteps thudded closer. Hinges squeaked ever so slightly as my closed door pushed open. I opened my mouth to scream.

Nothing came out.

The hulking figure paused in the doorway, then moved across my room. I stared, frozen in terror, my knuckles throbbing from my viselike grip on the comforter. I wanted to scream, to call for help, but my vocal cords refused to cooperate.

The figure kept his back toward me. He didn't seem to know that I was there, cowering in my narrow bed. I tried desperately not to breathe, not to make any noise.

Go away. Please, go away, I prayed.

He was dressed entirely in black. A black ski hat obscured his face. Black gloves covered his hands.

Why was he in my room?

89

Please, go away.

He stopped at my dresser and pushed aside my perfume bottles. His back still toward me, he extracted a thin flashlight from some pocket and shone it on a large box. A box I didn't recognize.

Did I have a box on my dresser? No, definitely not.

My eyes widened as he scooped jewelry from the box. Not my kind of cheap mall jewelry. Diamond necklaces. A ruby brooch. Bracelets glittering with sapphires and emeralds. Strands and strands of luminescent pearls. In seconds he'd emptied the contents of the box into a bulging sack.

My mind raced. Whose expensive jewelry was he stealing in my bedroom?

I blinked, trying to understand, and in that moment, he turned and faced my bed. He was coming for me.

No, please.

My voice still wouldn't cooperate, but I managed to release the covers and bolt upright in my bed.

Cold sweat trickled down my chest. My pajama top was soaked with my fear.

I swung my legs around, ready to race out the open door for the hall. Ready to dodge his hulking body.

He wasn't there.

Frantically I scanned my room. It's small—the smallest in the house. There's nowhere for a man to hide.

He was completely gone.

Yet I wasn't alone.

The spirit from the boardwalk hovered in my desk chair. I could barely see her. Her body shimmered in and out of focus. She regarded me, quaking on my bed, with an almost serene contentment.

My eyes found my clock. 5:12 a.m. How could that be? The man hadn't been in here for *three hours*. Or had he? Or was I dreaming?

The old woman remained in the chair. Her body grew more solid, and for the first time, I could make out a hint of her hands, gnarled like claws.

"You have it now," she murmured.

Every instinct cautioned me to shrink back, but I leaned closer to better hear her airy rasp.

"You have the key."

"Key?" I repeated, my voice suddenly working.

"Help me." With that, she disappeared too.

Chapter 9

Obviously, there was no way I was going back to sleep.

I turned on all my lights and changed my sweaty pajamas. I double-checked that my closet and under my bed were clear of anyone. Then I inspected my dresser. Everything was exactly how it had been when I went to bed last night. Perfume bottles all lined up. Nothing out of place.

Even stranger, my bedroom door remained completely closed.

I wrapped my arms around a stuffed pig that I used to hug a lot when I was younger and tried to make sense of what had happened.

The burglar had been a dream, I decided. A scary dream.

The spirit, I felt certain, had been here.

I need to talk to Lady Azura, I thought. I'd put it off long enough. Once again, I glanced at my clock. 6:02. It was too early to wake her.

I tried to read a book, but I couldn't make sense of the story. A half hour later, I heard my dad's sneakers pad down the stairs. He'd be going for his Sunday morning jog. He didn't notice that my lights were on.

I waited for the front door to click closed, then went downstairs, slapping my hand along the banister to make as much noise as possible. Maybe she'd think she woke up naturally, I hoped. Doubtful, though. Lady Azura was not a morning person.

Cautiously I pushed back the velvet curtains to her fortune-telling room. The scent of cinnamon candles greeted me. The heavy drapes along the front windows blocked the early morning sunlight. I wound my way around the table where she did readings and stood in front of another curtained doorway. This one led to her bedroom.

I debated turning around and watching TV until she woke. But that could be hours, and my dad would be back. The dream, the spirit, the visions at the boardwalk, Mystery Boy, and Miranda's dad tumbled about in my brain like a washing machine's spin cycle on overdrive. One, then another, each one competing for my attention.

I couldn't wait any longer.

Lady Azura slept on a satin pillowcase and with a satin eye mask. She wasn't easy to wake, but once I got her attention, she slipped into her white silk robe. She settled into one of the modern black-leather armchairs in the sitting area of her large room. She was ready to listen.

I started with the vintage jewelry and Buddy. "What's going on?" I asked.

She looked pale and tired, either because she didn't have her full face of makeup on or because I'd woken her so early. "What do *you* think is happening?"

"If I knew that, I wouldn't be here," I said.

Lady Azura didn't reply. She just waited.

I sighed. This was her way of teaching me. She wanted me to discover my abilities myself. She wanted me to be more in touch with my emotions and all that. She'd been saying that for the past five months I'd been coming to her for guidance.

"I think the visions have to do with the thing I'm

holding at the time," I ventured. "The dog's collar or the ring."

She nodded. "I think that's it too. It's wonderful."

"Wonderful?" Was she serious?

"Yes. There are many powers within us. They lie dormant until our body and our mind are ready to embrace and develop them. Thirteen tends to be a turning point. A time to unlock certain powers. This is the shift I saw." She clapped her hands together happily.

"I don't want another new power." I unclasped the chain from around my neck. "Here's this diamond or Herkimer-thingy back. I don't want it. I don't want to see things anymore."

She refused to take the crystal back. "The Herkimer diamond is not causing your psychometry. It is merely an agent to fine-tune your power. You saw the dog's owners before I gave you the crystal. With or without it, the power is within you."

"What did you call it?"

"Psychometry." Her dark eyes sparkled. "It's the ability to see the past through the handling of an object. Touching an object opens a window into the owner's world."

That made sense when I thought about the ring and the gambling woman, and the necklace and the hairdresser. Each woman had owned and worn the jewelry I'd tried on. But I'd also held the sandals and the headband and the metal dog figurine and hadn't seen anything. "It doesn't work all the time."

"No, it doesn't. I suspect it has to do with the emotional content of an item. Great emotion, happy or sad, contains potent energy, and energy is not stagnant. It transfers itself into the object it is closest to." She clicked her tongue. "I used to excel at psychometry in my younger days. Oh, Sara, you have so many exciting things to look forward to. This power is just the beginning."

"Beginning of wha—" I changed my mind. I'd deal with other powers later. "I don't want to touch things and see people's lives. I definitely didn't want to see my friend's dad screaming at her. It's embarrassing."

"You can control psychometry," she assured me. "Just like the mind reading. But unlike mind reading, which tends to invade privacy and lead to heartache, psychometry can be wonderful."

"How do I block it when I need to?" I asked. I

wasn't sure how wonderful this was going to be, but hearing Lady Azura say it wasn't bad did reassure me a little. She'd always been honest with me about my powers.

"When you pick up on an object's energy, when you sense the hum of vibrations coming off it, you can block out transmissions."

"How do I do that?"

"You must clear your mind. Completely. You must go into a state of blankness."

"You do that sometimes, don't you?" I'd often seen her lapse into a trancelike state.

She nodded. "Yes. You can too."

"What if I can't? Sometimes my brain won't shut up. There are always thousands of thoughts fighting for space in there."

"Nonsense." She waved her hand. "You can control anything with practice. We'll practice."

"Now? But . . ." I'd only begun to tell her about the visions from the objects. I hadn't gotten to the dream and the dead woman with the key.

Lady Azura walked over to the glass shelves that lined the wall above a low-slung white leather sofa.

Everything in her black-and-white bedroom area was extremely modern; she called it "art deco." She lifted a small glass bird from a collection of bird figurines.

"A hummingbird," she explained. "But the question is: whose hummingbird?"

She placed the bird in my hands. The handblown glass was a medley of greens. I cradled the bird, rubbing my fingers along its shiny surface. Its little body began to expel heat, warming my skin. The hot sensation traveled up my arms and spread throughout my body.

"Why is—" I stopped.

A man stood before me. Tall with thick gray hair and an even thicker gray mustache. He wore a blue chambray work shirt and khakis. He whistled the same four notes over and over. A birdcall, I realized.

Still whistling, he reached for a book wedged on a crowded bookshelf. As he tried to jiggle it loose, his elbow bumped one of many bird figurines on a nearby display shelf. He gasped, and my heart leaped as it tumbled toward the ground. Instinctively he dove forward, narrowly catching it before it smashed. He cradled the little bird in his hands.

The little green glass hummingbird.

"I saved you, number fifty-six," he said, relief flooding him—and me. He carefully placed the bird back on the shelf, lining it up between a ceramic dove and a glass cardinal.

His bird call morphed to the whistled tune of "Happy Birthday." "Let's see what new friend Zuri gives us tomorrow," he told his bird audience. His affection for Zuri ran through me.

"And?" Lady Azura said, pulling me back to the bedroom.

The man was gone. I placed the hummingbird back on the shelf. "He loved you," I said quietly. "This was your husband's hummingbird, and he called you Zuri, right?"

"Richard, yes."

Her husband, my great-grandfather, had been dead for twenty years. He'd been a college professor who studied birds. I described what I'd seen. Lady Azura explained that every year she'd bought Richard a bird figurine for his birthday. He called them by the number of the birthday year. She'd gotten the hummingbird for his fifty-sixth birthday. She gazed at me in wonder, looking ready to burst with excitement.

"You're happy I saw him, aren't you? That's so sweet!"

"No." She waved her hand, dismissing my silliness. "I visit with Richard all the time. Sweet man, but truthfully, he was kind of boring. No, I am happy about the incredible clarity of your vision. You have a gift, my child."

"You were going to teach me how *not* to have this gift." I was starting to panic. What if I saw something every time I touched a pencil, a glass, a computer, a remote control? I'd go crazy.

"How to block it, not get rid of it." She lifted a small ceramic blackbird off the shelf and placed it in my palm. "Now concentrate. Literally imagine you are putting up a wall between you and the object," she instructed. "Build that wall out of bricks, rocks, stone, or whatever it takes."

I closed my eyes. Heat started to seep from the bird. *No,* I thought. I chose rocks. Big rocks piled one on top of the other. Interlocking. Walling off the bird. Walling away the warmth.

My hands felt numb. Not warm. Not cold.

It was working.

I saw nothing but the wall. Rock balanced upon

rock. Then the rocks began to fade, and I couldn't hold back the laughter. It gurgled, then bubbled up from deep inside, flooding my veins.

I watched Lady Azura—a much younger Lady Azura—in the kitchen. Happy birthday balloons were tied to a chair. She scooped blackberry filling into a piecrust, then gently placed a tiny ceramic blackbird in the center, swimming in the fruit. Giggling to herself, she rolled out a sheet of pastry and covered the pie and the bird. As she crimped the edges and sliced two slits to allow the steam to escape while baking, she hummed a familiar melody.

What was it? Oh, yes! I recognized the song. I laughed again.

"Sara!" She shook my shoulder.

I blinked. Lady Azura stood by my side in her bedroom, not in the kitchen. She was old.

"You baked this blackbird into a pie, like the nursery rhyme." *She can be silly,* I thought.

She grinned. "Richard was sure surprised that year."

"The wall thing, it didn't work," I accused.

"Patience and practice," she said. "Let's do it again."

Bird after bird, I worked on blocking out Richard

and his feathered memories. It took a long, long time. I wanted to quit, but Lady Azura wouldn't let me. Finally I was able to hold a metal woodpecker and build a solid wall out of Legos, of all crazy things.

"You have the mind strength, you see? We'll continue constructing walls after breakfast. I'll make French toast," she offered, heading toward the door. She started whistling the blackbird rhyme, clearly happy with me.

"I didn't tell you everything."

She turned mid-whistle.

"There was a woman . . . and a dream." I described the dream and the woman's visit in great detail. Lady Azura asked question after question about the woman. What she wore. What she looked like. How she held herself.

I did the best I could. It'd been hard to see her and hard to remember exactly. "Why do you care so much? I mean, she looked like a stuffy old woman. Really preppy, with weird hands."

"Something very exciting is happening. Indeed, indeed." She hurried over to a mirrored dresser and began rummaging through the top drawer.

"What?"

"Where is it? Where is it?" she muttered, flinging key chains, cocktail napkins with notes scribbled on them in ink, a dried corsage that had turn black, and an assortment of business cards to the ground.

"What are you looking for?"

I got no answer as she dug through what I assumed was her junk drawer, but then again, all her drawers and closets bulged with eighty years' worth of clothes and trinkets.

"Now I get it!" I suddenly exclaimed. "Why you wouldn't donate your stuff."

"My energy. My memories. My secrets. At least, while I'm still breathing." She pulled out a silk scarf with a distinctive swirled pattern in peach and taupe. "Found it." She motioned me closer. "Hold on to an end."

"What is it?"

"A scarf. Quite expensive. An Italian designer. I hope I can still do this." She still grasped one end. I reached for the other. She placed her free hand over mine. "No walls this time," she murmured, eyes fluttering closed.

"Whose scarf is—" I sucked in my breath.

The tall woman entered a darkened room and switched on a lamp. She'd returned from somewhere fancy. Her black velvet dress reached down to the floor, and her signature pearls circled her neck. She looked much younger, with pale-blue eye shadow and brown hair in the same pixie cut.

"Louis!" Her screech made me jump. Shock and horror overwhelmed me as my eyes followed hers to an elegant, carved cherrywood dresser, where perfume bottles lay scattered and a lacquered jewelry box stood open.

And empty.

Her body shook with outrage. "Louis! We've been robbed!"

My eyes widened, bringing me back. I tried to steady my hand, which trembled so badly the scarf waved up and down like the parachute we used to crawl under during gym.

Lady Azura's eyes snapped open. "That's Irene. Did you recognize her?"

I nodded. She was the spirit from the boardwalk who had visited me in my room.

"Did you see her discover that her jewelry had been stolen?" Lady Azura's eyes sparkled as she glanced down at the scarf that still connected us. "Black dress. Open box. Calling for her husband."

"You saw it too?" Somehow we'd just shared the same vision. "So the robbery wasn't a dream?"

"Irene was my client long ago. I couldn't help her. I'd thought we were done." Lady Azura shook her head. "I guess we're not. Irene is back, but this time she's coming to you."

Chapter 10

That afternoon, on my way to Lily's, I reviewed everything Lady Azura had told me.

Irene Meyer had first come to her in 1987, looking for help. Lady Azura remembered that it was in April, because the daffodils were in bloom and she was arranging a bouquet in the front hall when Irene drove up in her fancy car. She remembered being startled by Irene's regal bearing. Her clients weren't usually wealthy. They were mostly the local workers and summer tourists in the sleepy shore town.

Irene was different.

She'd heard about Lady Azura through her housekeeper's cousin, who lived in Stellamar. Irene was from Harbor Isle, a nearby town of majestic, old shingled houses, and had been the victim of a robbery that year. Her jewels had been stolen, and the police had no leads. Her husband, Louis, trusted that the police would figure it out soon. Irene refused to wait. She wanted her jewels back—not because of their value, which was huge, but because she'd inherited most of them from her mother and grandmother. They were family heirlooms that she intended to pass down to her son. Family was very important to Irene.

She refused to let anyone rob her of that.

She'd brought Lady Azura a silk scarf that had been wrapped around a string of her pearls so they wouldn't get scratched. The thief would've touched the scarf to snatch the pearls. Lady Azura used psychometry several different times to try to discover the identity of the thief or the location of the jewels. She'd seen the man in black place the jewels in a pouch. But that was it. Try as she might, she could never pull any more information from the scarf.

The same scarf she'd kept in her drawer for all those years.

The scarf we'd both held on to this morning.

Disappointed, Irene left Lady Azura, vowing to track down her jewels another way. Lady Azura had never heard from her again, but she never forgot Irene. It bothered her that she hadn't been able to help. She'd really liked Irene.

If only she'd had the ability to delve deeper into the visions . . .

If only her power would've let her see more . . .

"You must finish what I started so many years ago," Lady Azura had said.

"Me? Why me?"

"Your grasp on psychometry is already better than mine ever was. Without us both holding the scarf and my tapping into your power, I'm no longer able to see anything. And I never absorbed the feelings the way I know you do."

"I have no idea how to help. Besides, she's dead and the jewelry's gone, so it doesn't matter anymore."

"It matters to Irene. She won't rest until she finds her jewels. Until *you* find her jewels."

I'd been here before. When the dead want something, need something, so they can stop roaming Earth in pain, they are relentless. Irene would keep coming. Upsetting me. Scaring me. Begging me.

"She talked about a key. She says I have a key, but

I don't." My head started to pound.

"Well," Lady Azura had said, as if it were the most rational thing in the world, "I guess it's time to find this mysterious key."

I realized I'd been standing on Lily's porch for a few minutes, lost in thought. Shaking my head to clear my thoughts, I knocked, and Lily immediately answered.

"I bought this for you," I said, handing Lily the little cast-iron dog once I was up in her room.

She squealed. "It looks just like Buddy! I love, love, love it!" She placed it on the shelf beside her dance trophies. Definitely a place of honor. "I'm going to call him Buddy Two."

Buddy 1 lay panting at her feet.

"I downloaded tons of training info. Buddy and I have been working nonstop." She lowered her voice and shielded her mouth so Buddy wouldn't see. "He's not very smart."

"Yikes. Isn't tomorrow shelter day?"

"Don't say that! It won't be. By tomorrow, Buddy will be able to fetch the newspaper from the driveway." She shoved a handful of old newspapers at me. "This is what we have to do."

She folded a section of newspaper and secured it with a piece of tape. Then she tucked a small dog treat inside the folded paper. She walked across the room and placed the paper close to the window. "Get the paper, Buddy! Get the paper!"

Buddy's ears perked up, and he scampered to the newspaper.

"He's doing it!" I cried.

Buddy nudged the paper with his nose, pushing it across the pink carpet.

"Get it, Buddy! Get it," Lily encouraged. "Use your mouth."

Buddy bent down, then used a combination of his nose and paw to shred the newspaper and extract the doggie treat. Swallowing it in one gulp, he gazed up at Lily expectantly, eager for more.

Lily sighed. "Been going like this all morning."

"He doesn't understand what 'get' means. Put the newspaper in his mouth when you say the command."

She tried that, but then Buddy refused to release the paper. We had to pry his tiny jaws off it. The newspaper dripped with his drool. Totally unreadable.

We tried rewarding him with the treat after he

grabbed the paper. He just waited for the treat, ignoring the newspaper entirely.

We tried attaching him to a leash, hiding a treat in the folded paper, releasing him to get it, and drawing him back like a canine yo-yo. It sort of worked the first few times; then we tried it with the full newspaper, not a few folded sheets.

"He's too small to grasp it." I pointed out the obvious when Buddy failed to lift the newspaper.

"He can do this if he tries. The sliced turkey Mom bought for lunch will motivate him." Lily left for the kitchen. I knew Lily. She wouldn't quit.

Buddy sprawled by my side on the floor between Lily and Cammie's beds. His eyes blinked rapidly, then closed. He breathed heavily, enjoying a nap before Sergeant Lily returned.

I stared at his green collar.

I could touch it right now and find out where he belongs, I thought. *I have the power to send him home.*

But there was Lily. She would be devastated if I did that.

But then there was the boy. Who was he? Where was he? And why couldn't I stop thinking about him?

One touch, I decided. Now that I knew what this power was, now that I knew it had a name, I'd be able to control it, to see the boy but shut it down before I saw anything that would ruin Lily's chances of keeping Buddy.

But . . .

I remembered Mystery Boy's eyes. His familiar eyes. I placed my hand on Buddy's collar, watching it rise and fall with his gentle breathing.

A man and a woman stood before me.

His hair was white, and he wore a light-blue golf shirt that matched his light-blue eyes. She was deeply tan and also white-haired, though she had dark eyes. She wore capri pants and a yellow blouse. She shielded her eyes with her hand and swiveled about, scanning the area.

"Buddy! Buddy!" A cry of barely controlled panic.

The smell of grease. French fries and burgers. And gasoline.

"Here, boy!" The man stuck two fingers into his mouth and let out a sharp whistle.

"Buddy!" The woman rose to her toes to better view the parking lot. Hundreds of cars. Gas pumps. A neon sign flashing REST STOP. "Where is he?"

The man rubbed his temples. Anxiety pumped through him—and through me. Buddy was lost.

Lost!

The man leaned against the trunk of a blue car with a blue, white, and gold license plate. A Lincoln College sticker flashed from the back window.

"Guess what I have, Buddy? Turkey!"

Buddy leaped to attention, nudging me back to reality.

Lily repeated the newspaper trick with the turkey— and with no better results.

I lay on Lily's carpet, staring at her ceiling. Who were the man and woman? Were they Buddy's owners? Was the boy? Or the twin little kids? The couple I had seen seemed too old to have young children, though I was sure they were all connected to Buddy. I couldn't make sense of all the visions. How many lives had Buddy touched?

"I could sooner train Joey's goldfish." Lily flopped onto her desk chair.

"That's not true." But it was. The Randazzo newspaper was not being delivered by Buddy anytime soon.

Lily flipped open her laptop and began clicking. "Maybe there's another trick. Something easier."

I wondered about the car. New Jersey had black numbers and letters on a yellow license plate. The man and woman weren't from here. I'd seen that license plate a lot, though. It was definitely from a nearby state.

"I could teach him to put away Cammie's Barbies. My mom hates how they're scattered everywhere." Lily jumped up in search of a doll.

"Can I go on your computer?"

"Sure. Buddy, look who I have!" She waved a one-armed Barbie at the dog.

I Googled Lincoln College. The website for a school in Pennsylvania appeared. Brick buildings and a clock tower. It looked pretty but didn't tell me anything about Buddy. But what was I expecting? It's not like he'd be sitting on the page as the college mascot or something.

"Fetch, Buddy!"

Pennsylvania. The blue, white, and gold license plate was from Pennsylvania, I remembered.

Lots of people from there came to the Jersey shore. Was Buddy from Pennsylvania?

I watched him trot around the room with Barbie dangling from his mouth. How did that help me? Pennsylvania was a huge state.

"Drop it, Buddy. Drop the doll." Lily squatted next to him, trying to pull Barbie to safety.

I could touch his collar again. See something else about him.

Freeing Barbie, Lily nuzzled her face in Buddy's fur. "It's okay, boy," she murmured. "We'll get it. I promise."

I turned back to the computer. *Leave it alone,* I told myself. *Just because I have these powers doesn't mean I should use them to mess things up for Lily.*

I didn't have to use them ever again. For anyone.

But what about Irene? Lady Azura's story replayed in my mind. Who was Irene really?

I Googled her name. The first entry was an obituary. I knew she was dead, but my eyes went wide when I saw the date on the article. April 26. She'd died two weeks ago.

I skimmed the obituary. It was long, more of a full-length article. As I read on, I understood why. She had been really rich. She and her husband, Louis, had started the biggest Christmas tree light business in the country. Her husband had died years before. She was on the board of many charities and traced her family back to the Pilgrims on the *Mayflower*. The coolest part was that she was really spiritual. She held séances instead of dinner parties, visited the Dalai Lama in Tibet, and took tai chi classes. The obituary referred to her as "beloved" and "eccentric." She sounded like a cool lady. No wonder Lady Azura had liked her so much.

"Who's that?" Lily stood by my side and pointed to the picture of Irene on the screen.

"An old client of Lady Azura's. She just died." I typed "Irene Meyer + Lady Azura" into the search bar.

Nothing appeared.

"What about fortune-teller, instead of Lady Azura?" Lily suggested.

No sooner had I hit enter than a short article titled "Heiress Employs Local Fortune-Teller in Search for Jewels" opened onto the screen.

Lily scooted next to me on the chair, and we read the article together.

Irene Meyer, prominent Harbor Isle resident, is trying everything and anything to recover the precious family heirlooms that were stolen from her house on the night of November 23. While police are still investigating, Mrs. Meyer has sought the assistance of a local fortune-teller who goes by the name of Lady Azura. Lady Azura runs a small establishment in nearby Stellamar and has been credited with the return of five-year-old Sabrina Selez, who went missing from her yard last June, and for locating elderly John Feringa, who wandered away from the Seaside Assisted Living Facility last March. Mrs. Meyer is hoping that Lady Azura's extraordinary abilities will help locate her stolen jewels.

"Lady Azura can do stuff like that?" Lily's voice was a hush. "Find people? And things?"

"I don't know," I admitted. "She's never told me about tracking down a missing child and a confused old person. That's really cool."

"Is she going to track down Buddy's owners?" Lily gripped my arm. "Is that why you're looking at that article? Are you going to have her do that?"

"What? No way!"

"I'd understand if you asked her. You know, if she could really find his owners . . . it's just that, well, I was hoping that—"

"I didn't ask." I cut Lily off. "I would never do that. In fact, she thinks Buddy should stay here with you."

"She does?"

I nodded. "She thinks Buddy showing up here is fate. That it was meant to be."

Lily grinned. "Have I told you lately how awesome she is?" Her eyes skimmed the article again. "She's really cool, isn't she? I've never heard of anyone with psychic abilities who could find missing people. Have you?"

Have I? Could I count myself?

If Lady Azura had the ability to do such great things, did I, too? Was that why Irene's spirit had sought me out? Was I the one who could find her missing jewels?

"No," I told Lily. "Hey, let's keep working with Buddy. I want him to get it before I go. I don't have much time. There are some things I need to do at home."

I needed to see what my powers could really do.

Chapter 11

The man in black came back that night. The jewel thief.

He hunched in a straight-backed chair, facing the corner of the room. I craned my neck for a better view. He was so close. If I could get him to turn, I could see his face.

His arms moved. I could make out a screwdriver in one hand. In the other, he held an object. I squinted in the dimness. What was it? His arm twisted as he loosened a screw in the object.

He rested the screwdriver in his lap, as the object neatly broke down the middle into two parts. I watched in silent fascination as he extracted a shiny key from his pocket and wrapped it in what looked to be cotton. He tucked it into half of the object, then replaced the screw with the screwdriver, making the object whole again.

Raising the object, he gave it a shake and listened. No noise. The cotton prevented the key from rattling. He shook it again, and at that moment, a car passed by outside. Its headlights crossed the window, illuminating the scene. I know I should have looked at the man's face. I should've tried to identify the thief, but all I could see was the object he held up.

A small cast-iron dog.

The car headed down the street, taking the light with it. In the shadows, the man stood. He opened a closet door. He rummaged about inside, then reached up high and slid the metal dog containing the cotton-wrapped key far back onto the top shelf.

Satisfied, he slammed the door closed.

Thwump!

I sat up straight, fighting the sheets tangled around my body. My sweaty pajamas clung to my skin. My heart raced. I searched my room for him.

A dream, I told myself. *It was just a dream.*

I exhaled and listened to the familiar sounds of the house. Floorboards creaked as the spirit in the second-floor sitting room paced. He did that every night.

It was still dark outside. My clock glowed. 2:58.

I had seen the jewel thief hide a key inside the little dog I'd bought on the boardwalk. I remembered how I'd been drawn to the dog. As if I'd been meant to buy it.

I waited in my bed for Irene to appear. She'd appeared last time I had a dream about the thief. This time I was ready to talk to her. But she didn't show.

I found a sweatshirt, tugged it over my head, and went downstairs. Lady Azura was waiting for me.

"I made hot chocolate for you, too." She pointed at a cup on the table. "I sensed your turmoil."

I curled into the chair and related my dream to Lady Azura.

"This is incredible." Her voice rose with excitement. "The thief placed the key inside the dog and then hid the dog in a closet. The contents of that closet somehow ended up for sale at Bargain on the Boardwalk. This is the key Irene meant. Hurry, Sara, get the little dog, and we'll open it!"

I started to go back upstairs, then stopped. "I don't have it."

"What?"

"I gave it to Lily yesterday. It was a present."

"You must get it back."

"It's the middle of the night now. I'm going to have to wait until after school tomorrow." I pushed a melting marshmallow with my tongue. "When we get the key, then what? What does it open?"

"I don't know, but I suspect the key was used to lock up the jewels."

"Irene told me about the key. She said it opened"—I tried to recall—"forty-three. What's forty-three?"

Lady Azura shrugged. "We'll need to ask her."

"I found out that she just died two weeks ago." I told her about the obituary I'd read.

"So she died recently. That explains a lot. In death, unfinished business is often resolved." Lady Azura stood. "Let's call Irene," she said.

"Call her?" I stood too.

"Call her back from the dead," Lady Azura made her way toward her fortune-telling room. "We will have a séance." I watched in wonder as she prepared the room. Curtains drawn. Lights dimmed. Candles lit. Crystal bell waiting on the table. My hand rested on the Herkimer diamond around my neck.

"Sit," she commanded. She sat in her big armchair, and I perched on a chair across the large, round table from her. She reached for my right hand.

In the flickering glow of the candlelight, Lady Azura closed her eyes and had me do the same. "Feel the flow of energy. From me to you, you to me, and back again. A never-ending chain."

I envisioned energy to be a cord that connected us, through our hands, through our bodies, to our souls.

"Picture Irene."

I saw the regal woman. Pearls and velvet dress.

The bell chimed four times. "We ring this bell to the four corners of the Earth. To the four seasons of the year. To the four directions of the wind. Move among us, Irene. Come to us, Irene. Irene."

My left foot began to tingle. Slightly at first. Something was happening.

"Irene. Irene."

The air turned warm. Stifling.

"Irene."

Not enough air for everyone. The room felt crowded. Someone was here.

The doorway curtain behind me swished. I opened my eyes as a shadow fell across the table.

"Irene?" Lady Azura called. "Is that you, Irene?"

Chapter 12

"Who's Irene?"

The voice was deep and male. For a moment, I feared we'd called up the jewel thief. Then he stepped forward.

My dad.

Hair flattened from sleeping on his right side, he looked back and forth between me and Lady Azura. He held a large black umbrella.

"Is it raining?" I asked lamely.

"I thought someone had broken in. It was the first thing I could grab in the foyer." He reached back and flipped the light switch. "What on earth is going on here?"

Lady Azura seemed suddenly very interested in the age spots on her hands.

"We were having a séance," I explained. "We're trying to contact an old client of Lady Azura's who just died. She needs our help. Well, we kind of need her help too."

Beads of sweat appeared on Dad's forehead. It was warm in the room, but that wasn't why.

"At three in the morning?"

"It's important," I said. "It's an old mystery, and I had a dream and we may be close to solving it."

He seemed about to say something, then changed his mind. My powers were still new to him, and he was treading lightly.

Instead he turned to Lady Azura. "You know better. At least, I should hope you do. Sara is a child. She has school in only a few hours. I'm not sure how I feel about this séance stuff, but I do know that it is definitely not happening in the middle of the night on a school night."

Lady Azura nodded. "I'm sorry, Mike." I wondered if she really was.

"Sara, up to bed now."

"But, Dad, I felt her here—"

"Now."

I knew that tone. There was no arguing. I stood to go.

Tomorrow, Lady Azura mouthed.

"Okay, what's with the gloves?"

I looked down at my thin black gloves. "You don't like them?"

"I don't understand them," Lily confessed as we walked home from school on Monday afternoon. "Are you in the Tour de France, or is it some eighties Madonna look where you forgot to cut off the fingertips?"

"Neither. It's my own fashion statement. I thought they looked good with this outfit."

That wasn't true, although I didn't think they looked totally awful with the black pants and neon pink shirt I wore. But then again, I'm not exactly the most fashionable girl in the world. I usually rely on Lily for that stuff.

But I couldn't tell Lily the real reason I'd worn the gloves to school. I couldn't tell her that I was afraid to touch things. Anything. This morning at breakfast, I'd touched Lady Azura's bread box and saw a young version of her trying to stop a little girl from crying by making a peanut butter sandwich. Then I'd touched the front door handle and was transported into the life of one of Lady Azura's clients, the strange woman who always wore a black raincoat. All the mental walls I tried to build crumbled.

I couldn't block out the psychometry today. I think maybe it was because I was so tired. Lady Azura was still fast asleep when I left, so I couldn't ask her what to do. Gloves were the only answer.

They actually worked. Plus, Avery told me she thought I looked "fierce." "Maybe I'll start a new trend," I suggested.

"Or not." Lily smiled at me, amused for the first time today. Today was Shelter Day.

We approached her front walk slowly. Even with her three brothers and a sister inside, the house would feel quiet without Buddy. Lonely.

Then we heard him.

Barking and scampering excitedly on the other side of the door.

"He's still here!" Lily cried, pushing her way into the house and scooping up the little dog. Buddy licked her face. His tail never stopped wagging.

"Hello, Lily? Sara, is that you, too?" Mrs. Randazzo called from the kitchen.

"Mom! Buddy's here, does that mean—"

"It just means we're waiting for your dad to get home, Lily. The plan is still to take Buddy to the shelter later. I'm sorry, sweetie."

Lily's face fell.

I didn't know what to say. "What if his owners never come? What does the shelter do then?" I dared to ask as Buddy followed me and Lily up to her room.

Lily sprawled face-first onto her bed. "I hope they find him a good home."

"It won't be as good as your home."

"Right? It's so unfair." She sounded as if she was barely holding back tears.

I dropped my book bag on the floor by the desk and watched Buddy curl up by the foot of Cammie's bed. Did he feel as good as I did when I slept here? Part of the family too?

Switching on Lily's iPod, I turned up the speaker volume. Pop music filled the room. I hoped to drown out the depressing silence. After one song played through, I reached up to the shelf over her desk. "Listen, I need to borrow Buddy Two. Just for a little while."

"What?" Lily raised her head. "You gave him to me. You can't take back a present."

"I'm not taking him back. Just borrowing him overnight."

"Oh my God! My parents take Buddy One away, and now you're taking Buddy Two! What's going on?"

"It's not like that." My timing couldn't have been worse. "He's broken. My dad will fix him for you. I'll bring him back tomorrow."

"He looks fine to me." She stood, lifted the heavy little iron dog from the shelf, and examined it.

"I promise I'll bring him back."

"Yeah, well, my parents promised that some-day we'd get a dog. Then the best dog in the world appears, and do we get to keep him? No!" Lily held on to the dog tightly. "Buddy Two may be the only dog I'll ever have. My only reminder of the real Buddy." She clutched Buddy 2 and reached down to pet Buddy 1, who wagged his tail by her side.

Now what? There was no way I could convince her to hand over the metal dog, especially when she was already so upset.

But the key was inside. I was sure of it. I needed to get it out.

"Knock, knock." Lily's mom poked her head into the room.

"Hi," I said.

Lily ignored her.

"Lily"—she crouched next to her daughter—"I just spoke to your dad on the phone. Actually, we've been talking about this a lot. All week. I'm not promising anything, but we've seen how good you've been with Buddy. Your brothers, too." She ran her fingers through Buddy's fur. "Maybe the shelter is not the right place for Buddy."

"Do you mean we're going to keep—"

Mrs. Randazzo held up her hand, stopping Lily. "I don't mean anything. All I mean is we're going to examine different options. We're going to have a family meeting tonight. A discussion." She stood, and Lily did too.

"What options?" Lily placed Buddy 2 on the edge of her desk and eagerly faced her mother.

"That's what we'll discuss. Maybe there's something we're missing. Let's wait for your dad, okay?"

"Mommy!" Cammie wailed from downstairs.

Mrs. Randazzo headed toward her. Lily hurried along beside her mom, peppering her with questions. Buddy followed too.

I stood alone in Lily's room.

Would she get to keep Buddy? I couldn't tell.

I raised the cast-iron dog to my ear and shook it hard. Did I hear something rattling faintly inside? Or was I wishing I did?

I ran my hand over its body. A seam ran down its middle, and on its stomach I spied a tiny metal screw. I would need a screwdriver to open it.

"Come on, Buddy. Let's go back to Sara!" Lily called. I heard the optimism in her voice. I could also hear her footsteps growing closer.

It was wrong. Totally wrong, I knew that. But before I could debate it with myself, I buried Buddy 2 deep in my book bag, slung it over my shoulder, and hurried into the hall.

I'll bring Buddy Two back tonight, I promised myself. *I'll pretend he fell into my bag by mistake.*

I met Lily on the stairs. "My stomach kind of hurts, and I promised Lady Azura I'd be home after school to help her," I said. Neither was a lie. "Text me after the family meeting, okay?"

"Okay." Lily watched me head out the front door.

My book bag felt unusually heavy, and I did feel sick. I had just stolen from my best friend.

We couldn't open it.

I tried every screwdriver Dad kept in the shed, and none would budge the screw. "It's rusted shut."

Lady Azura regarded the metal dog sitting on the table in her fortune-telling room. "We will have to wait for your father."

I glanced at the clock on my phone. How long until Lily discovered I'd taken Buddy 2?

"Shall we pick up from last night? Call back Irene?" She began to ready the room.

I helped, but my mind was on Lily. Would she buy the dropping-in-my-bag-by-accident story? I doubted it.

Lady Azura began the séance, rang the crystal bell, chanted, and called to Irene.

Should I tell Lily the truth about Irene? About my powers?

I wasn't paying attention. Not to Lady Azura, not to the tingling that ran up my leg, not to the temperature of the room. Irene completely startled me when she appeared alongside me. Shimmering. Still no hands. Barely visible. Yet here.

Lady Azura told of the man in black and the key.

Irene knew this already. "The man . . . the man who stole from . . . my gardener . . . Erik." Her voice was as faint as her body. Lady Azura gripped my hands tighter as if to heighten the connection.

"Your gardener did it," Lady Azura repeated.

"Erik passed too . . . years ago. We met here . . . he told me . . ."

I wondered where *here* was.

"And your jewels?" Lady Azura asked. She remained trancelike as she spoke.

"Erik . . . locked up in a box . . . key."

"We have the key."

"Seatight. Tell Thomas to go to Seatight." For a moment her pearls glowed, and then she was gone. I felt the air return to the room.

Lady Azura and I released our grip and took deep breaths.

"Who is Thomas?" we both said at the same time.

"Everything's jumbled." Lady Azura leaned back in her big chair. "Irene had her family jewelry stolen by a man dressed in black."

"Who turned out to be Erik the gardener. He died, and then he confessed his crime to Irene after she died too. Although I'm not sure where they had this conversation."

"That doesn't matter. We know Erik locked up the jewels someplace with a key," Lady Azura continued. "And that key, we think, is hidden inside this rusted metal dog."

"Which for some reason looks like the dog Lily's brothers happened to find when I was over their house."

"Exactly." She nodded. "The key opens a box with the number forty-three, where I presume the jewels are hidden. We are supposed to give the key to someone named Thomas."

"But we can't get the key out. We don't where box forty-three is, and we don't know who Thomas is."

"Exactly." Lady Azura's eyes clouded over. "I fear I have failed again. Irene's jewels may stay missing forever, and there's nothing either of us can do."

Chapter 13

I sat on the dusty attic floor, staring at the black wardrobe trunk. I was supposed to be in my room doing my homework while we waited for Dad. Lady Azura had gone to lie down. She was frustrated that we couldn't help Irene.

I unbuckled the latches and pried the trunk apart. Inhaling the smell of my mom, I surrounded myself with her dress bags, pulling them around me like an embrace.

"Do you know what I can do?" I asked.

I suspected she didn't. Lady Azura said my mother hadn't had powers herself. I wondered what she would've thought about me had she lived.

I wanted her to be proud of me. Would she be?

I'd lied to Lily about Buddy 1 and Buddy 2.

A dead woman wanted me to find her stolen jewels.

She gave me clues, yet I didn't know where to look.

If I unzipped a bag and took out a dress, my mother would come back. She'd tell me what to do. How to make everyone happy.

If I have to have these powers, I thought, *all I want is for them to make things good for people.* Otherwise, what was the point?

I counted the dresses again. Fifteen. Fifteen chances to see my mom. No, fourteen. I'd used one already. I didn't know for sure, but I suspected that was how it worked. One dress, one glimpse.

I had to choose wisely.

I reached out . . . and slid the trunk closed.

Not today.

I didn't need her today.

I didn't need séances with spirits.

I didn't need to touch an object to get answers.

Suddenly I had an idea how I could help Irene. Just me, Sara Collins, with no paranormal help.

All I needed was my computer.

I made my way up to my room and booted up my computer. Then I stared at the keyboard, unsure how to begin.

"She had a son," Lady Azura had once told me. She wanted to pass on her jewels on to her son. Could Thomas be her son?

I typed "Thomas Meyer" into the search bar. Over seven thousand hits appeared. "Popular name," I said, scrolling through them.

Nothing looked right. Businessman from Germany. Poet in Arizona. *Maybe I'm wrong,* I thought. *Maybe Thomas is someone else. A friend? The police officer?*

My finger paused, and I stared at the twenty-fourth name listed on the screen. *Thomas Meyer, Dean of Students.*

The website was Lincoln College in Pennsylvania.

What were the chances?

I opened the site and clicked on Thomas Meyer's biography. He'd been educated in New Jersey. A formal photo showed a white-haired man in a dark suit.

"That's him," I said aloud.

I couldn't believe it. The man I'd seen at the rest stop, looking for Buddy, was named Thomas Meyer.

Were Buddy and Irene connected?

It didn't take long to track down a phone number for Thomas Meyer at the college. My hand trembled as

I woke Lady Azura from her nap and handed her the scrap of paper. "It's Thomas's number."

Lady Azura went into the kitchen to call him. I stayed behind.

Did Thomas have anything to do with Buddy? I wondered. Or had that rest stop vision really been about the key and Irene? Had I gotten them confused somehow?

The bad feeling I'd had when I left Lily's house grew worse. What had I done? Lily probably would forgive me for taking Buddy 2 away, but if she found out I had searched out and called a man who would take Buddy 1 away, that would be bad. End-of-a-friendship bad.

"You found him, Sara." Lady Azura returned, beaming. "He is Irene's son."

Was that good? I wasn't sure.

"Luckily, he remembered hearing his mother talk about me, otherwise I am sure he would have hung up. He is going to meet with us."

"Here?"

"Yes. In a couple of hours. It turns out his daughter and his grandchildren still live in the family home in Harbor Isle. He has another daughter who lives in Ocean Heights. He's used to coming down this way."

"Did he mention a dog?"

"No. Of course, neither did I. One thing at a time, my child." She touched the silk turban wrapped around her head. "I need to let down my hair and change my clothes. We're having company."

The doorbell rang two hours later. Thomas Meyer and his wife entered our foyer just as Dad came through the back kitchen door.

They both looked just as they had in my vision. Thomas, with his light, bright-blue eyes, and Helen, with her darker skin and coffee-colored eyes.

Lady Azura tried to explain everything to Dad and the Meyers. She told them that Irene had told her about a hidden key, "the key that opens the forty-three," and how that would lead them to the missing jewels. She didn't mention me or my visions or the psychometry, except to say that I had bought the cast-iron dog at the Bargains on the Boardwalk as a present for my friend, and that was where she believed the key was hidden. I knew she had to leave me out of it, but part of me wished I could join in the conversation and let them know how I had helped. How Irene had come to me.

Dad and Thomas Meyer asked a lot of questions, but I had trouble paying attention. The man and woman I'd seen frantic at a rest stop were now sitting at my kitchen table, smiling and marveling at the story Lady Azura was telling them. How strange was that?

Neither Lady Azura nor I mentioned Buddy. It wasn't a plan or anything. He just never came up.

"Well, I guess it's my turn to lend a hand," Dad said, surveying the array of screwdrivers on the table. He went out to the shed and returned with a spray can. "This lubricant will loosen the rust."

He alternated between the spray can and the screwdriver, working on the rusted screw with the patience of a bonsai artist. The four of us watched nervously. Would he be able to open it? Would the key be inside?

"It's been such a strange month," Thomas Meyer said suddenly. "My mother died a couple of weeks ago. She'd been sick for a long time. In some ways it was a relief to no longer see her in pain."

"What was wrong with her?" I asked.

"Cancer. It started as bone cancer in her hands, at the joints and in her wrists. It did terrible things to her hands. It eventually spread."

That explained her hands.

"We've spent so much time down this way lately," Helen mused. "We've been upset about Irene, so we've visited a lot with our daughters and their families. Our one daughter is single and lives in Ocean Heights. The other is married and lives in Harbor Isle with her family. Just a few exits down on the parkway."

"We were here not even two weeks ago, pulled over at the Stellamar rest stop, and we lost our dog. He ran away."

"That's awful," my dad said. He didn't know the connection either.

I couldn't say anything. All I could think of was Lily.

"Buddy does that, runs away." Helen shook her head. "Tom and I haven't been very good with that dog. He's a frisky one. He used to be our grandchildren's pet."

"What happened?" Lady Azura asked.

My heart had dropped to my knees. Lily would have to give Buddy back.

"Our daughter got Buddy as a puppy for the family, then discovered she was horribly allergic to the dog. Hives everywhere. She couldn't live with him, but our three grandkids were so attached. Tom and I offered to take Buddy in. Our grandkids visited with him at our house on the weekends."

"Sounds like a good plan." My dad gave a grunt and twisted the screwdriver.

"Except Buddy needs to be with an active, young family. We are too old for that dog. My knees are bad, and Tom has back problems. We can't chase after him." Helen sighed. "Whenever he's run off, we've been lucky to find him."

"Not this time," Thomas said. "Buddy's gone, and our grandkids are crushed. Even worse, we had taken off his ID tags because the jingling was bothering us in the car. You have no idea the guilt we feel." He pointed to the figurine. "Weirdest thing, don't you think, Helen?"

At that moment, Dad pulled the screw out of the dog's belly. We all held our breaths. He pulled the two halves of the dog apart. A wad of cotton tumbled to the table. Inside was a small silver key.

Thomas Meyer turned the key over several times. "So this is the key that opened forty-three?" Thomas wondered aloud as he studied the key. "But what is forty-three?"

"It looks like a key to a safe-deposit box. The kind they have at banks," my dad said slowly.

"But what bank?" Thomas asked.

"The gardener lived in Jefferson, right next to Harbor Isle," Helen said.

Thomas sighed. "Jefferson has dozens of banks."

"Is there one called Seatight?" I asked.

"Box forty-three is at Seatight Bank," Lady Azura announced with conviction before I could say it.

As the adults inspected the key and talked about the bank, I slipped out the back door. I had no choice. I had to tell Lily. Leaning against the rusted metal chair on the small patio, I pulled out my cell phone.

CAN U COME OVER? I texted.

NOT NOW. OUT WALKING BUDDY, was her reply.

I could hear Thomas Meyer's booming voice thanking Lady Azura. He'd be going soon. I couldn't let him go without his dog. Plus, I didn't think Lady Azura would keep it a secret for much longer.

NOW!!!! COME NOW & BRING BUDDY!!!!!!!

WHATS UP?

YOU'LL SEE WHEN U GET HERE.

I felt bad not telling her, but I was afraid she

wouldn't show up if I did. I couldn't totally shock her, though. I had to intercept her on the front porch.

When I returned to the kitchen to cut through to the front, I overheard Thomas talking to my dad. "We weren't the right people for Buddy. I feel as if I failed the little guy. He deserved a house with loving, energetic kids."

I stopped, and for the first time in a long time, the whirlwind of ideas and fears twirling through my brain slowed, and I knew exactly how to make everyone happy. "I have an idea—"

I didn't get to finish.

"Buddy!" Thomas Meyer bellowed.

"You found our dog!" Helen cried.

Lily stood in the kitchen doorway, holding Buddy's leash. Her eyes darted frantically between the man and woman who'd crowded around her to hug Buddy. Then she found me. Her look of confusion turned to betrayal.

"How could you?"

Tears streamed down her cheeks. She dropped Buddy's leash and raced out the open front door.

Chapter 14

"Stop, Lily! Wait!"

Lily increased her speed, refusing to look back. She bounded down the porch steps and took off toward her house.

I chased after her as fast as I could, calling her name.

Mr. and Mrs. Randazzo were in their front yard, pruning rosebushes. Lily flung herself into her mother's arms. "Buddy! She took Buddy," she sobbed.

Her parents turned to stare at me.

I would've felt horrible, except I had an idea. A great idea.

"You need to come with me. All of you," I said.

I dragged Lily and her parents back into my house. I introduced them to the Meyers. Mr. and Mrs.

Randazzo were polite. Lily refused to talk to them or to me. Buddy was beside himself with excitement, scampering between the Meyers and Randazzos.

"I have an idea." I turned to the Meyers. "Lily and her family have taken really good care of Buddy. They love him, and he loves being with them. Anyone would. They're the most welcoming and caring family ever. And they have five kids. Five loving, energetic kids."

Everyone was staring at me now. I hoped this would work.

"Mr. Meyer, you said how Buddy was too frisky. How he keeps getting away from you and your wife. You kept him so your grandkids could still see him and play with him." I took a deep breath. "The Randazzos live really close to your daughter's family. What if you let them keep Buddy, and they promised to let your grandkids visit whenever they wanted? Kind of a shared-dog-between-two-families thing?"

For a moment, no one spoke.

Mr. and Mrs. Randazzo seemed to be sending each other silent messages. So were Mr. and Mrs. Meyer.

Then, all at once, everyone agreed.

Lily whooped with joy. She hugged her parents,

my dad, the Meyers, and even me. She saved the biggest hug of all for Buddy.

Her dog.

"The queen of cups," I said.

Lady Azura held up another card.

"The Empress." I flipped to lie on my stomach on the front porch. "I'm getting good at knowing the tarot cards."

"You are." She smiled down at me from the porch swing. I could barely see her face under her large sun hat. "Next we will work on their meanings."

Even though school had ended for the day, Lady Azura and I had our own lessons. Thursdays were tarot days. Yesterday we worked on blocking out the psychometry. I got really good at building those walls. I didn't have to wear gloves to school today. There were just a few days left in the school year. I wondered if I'd need the gloves at all next year.

"Lady Azura!" Lily barreled down the street. Buddy ran alongside, tugging at his leash. "Lady Azura, you're famous!"

I sat as they scampered up the porch steps. Buddy

slobbered my face with kisses.

"Look!" Lily waved the newest issue of the *Stellamar Sentinel*. "Check out the front page!"

"Shouldn't Buddy be bringing us the paper?" I joked.

"Buddy doesn't have to do tricks anymore." Lily nuzzled his neck. "Buddy can just be Buddy."

"Oh. Look, there I am." Lady Azura pointed to her photo. The headline screamed, MEYER FAMILY GETS STOLEN JEWELS BACK, THANKS TO LOCAL FORTUNE-TELLER.

Lily and I gathered close. We read together about how Lady Azura's psychic abilities and connection with the dead led her to discover the key that opened a safe-deposit box at Seatight Bank, where the thief had stashed the family's jewels.

"They're saying it's all because of you," Lily told Lady Azura.

"Nonsense." She waved Lily away.

"Mr. Meyer is so happy. He says that having his mother's jewelry back helps soothe the pain of her death." Lily turned to her. "Everyone in town is talking about you."

"Nonsense," Lady Azura repeated. "Besides,

Stellamar is a small town. This is news here, but nowhere else."

"Actually, you may be wrong about that." My dad had parked his car in the narrow driveway alongside the house and was now mounting the porch steps with his smartphone outstretched.

"The article has gone viral. News sources all over the country have picked up the story. Everyone wants to meet the all-knowing Lady Azura."

Just then the phone inside Lady Azura's fortune-telling room started to ring. We heard it through the open window. It rang and rang. No sooner had it stopped than it began to ring again.

"We are living with a celebrity," Dad declared.

"Nonsense." Lady Azura raised her penciled eyebrows at me. I knew she was secretly pleased. Being able to help Irene after all those years meant a lot to her.

She'd told me privately how grateful she was to me. How proud she was.

"No one cares about old people. The fascination with me will be a local blip. Gone in a flash," she said now.

I gazed at the stories flooding Dad's screen. I had a

feeling that Lady Azura was wrong. Her life was about to change. Big-time.

"Are you going to answer?" Lily asked. The phone continued to ring.

"Not now. Maybe after four."

"Four?"

"Four is hot chocolate time," I informed her. "The Queen of England has tea at four. We have hot chocolate. Want to help me make it?"

Lily handed Buddy's leash to my dad and followed me into the kitchen.

"I'm sorry again that I took Buddy Two even though you told me not to," I said when we were alone. I had apologized earlier, but I still felt bad.

"Why didn't you just tell me that Lady Azura knew there was a key inside? I would've just given him to you."

I shrugged. "I didn't know how to explain it all. Are you mad?"

"No! I got to keep the best dog in the world, and you did that!" Lily had been so happy all week. "Can I have Buddy Two back, or did Mr. Meyer take him?"

"He's in Lady Azura's room. He's all yours."

I hurried into the fortune-telling room. Buddy 2 sat on a shelf beside gemstones, a bowl of dried herbs, and a doll with a porcelain face that I knew had belonged to Lady Azura as a child. It was given to her by her grandmother.

How many secrets did this doll hold? If I touched it, I could see Lady Azura as a child. Even see her grandmother. I could learn things that she hadn't told me. Things she might not remember.

I reached my hand out. . . .

I had the power to reveal secrets.

I thought of my mother's dresses, hidden away upstairs. They contained precious glimpses into her life. How would I feel if someone else intruded on those secrets, if someone pushed back the shades and peeked through my window?

I'd be angry.

I pulled my hand away. I wouldn't do that to Lady Azura.

I turned, then noticed a photo on one of the side tables. I bent for a closer look. Lady Azura had framed a photo of the Meyer family that Thomas had given her. Buddy barked outside. Lily rattled cups in the kitchen. My attention was on the photo.

Irene sat in the center. Frail but still regal and wearing her pearls. Thomas and Helen stood on one side of her. Their daughter and her husband stood on the other side. Three kids knelt in the front row. The two blond six-year-old twins, whose names were Ben and Rachel, and a blond thirteen-year-old boy.

My Mystery Boy.

They said his name was Mason.

I couldn't stop staring at him.

Even through the photo, his eyes drew me in. Called to me. Those piercing green eyes. The eyes with secrets.

He wasn't like other boys.

I sucked in my breath. Soon he would be here, visiting his dog at Lily's house, and I would meet him. I had the weirdest feeling that was what Buddy, Irene, and the key were really all about. A way to bring me and Mason together.

Something bigger was still to come.

Want to know what happens to Sara next?

Here's a sneak peek at the next book in the series:

Kindred Spirits

"Suddenly, the curtain moved all by itself."

The late June sun found its way onto the front porch. I squinted into the glare at my best friend. "How?"

Lily Randazzo shrugged. "No one was standing anywhere near the window. And it was closed, so it wasn't a breeze that moved it."

Lily's voice grew quiet. "Everyone in room seventeen of the Spalding Inn sensed what was happening. Mr. Spalding was there, in that very room, pushing back the curtain and looking out the window. He was staring at the pond where he had drowned fifty years ago."

"Drowned?" I repeated. "Wait, is Mr. Spalding . . . dead?"

"He's d-d-dead?" Lily's five-year-old sister, Cammie, stuttered.

"Totally dead," Lily confirmed. "Now he's a ghost trapped in the inn."

"Ghosts are scary." Cammie tugged their dog Buddy closer.

"Even scarier," Lily continued, "was when Mr. Spalding's ghost pulled down the window shade. Right after he did that, there was this supercreepy wailing noise that sounded like it was coming from within the walls and from under the floors. Everyone was so freaked out. . . ."

"What was it?" Cammie asked. The color drained from her normally rosy cheeks.

"The ghost of Mr. Spalding was crying out in pain and frustration!" Lily explained, as if it were the most natural thing in the world.

"Did you help him?" Cammie grasped Buddy tightly.

Lily gently tugged one of her sister's black braids. "No, silly. I wasn't there. I was watching a movie."

"What movie?" I asked.

"*The Haunting at the Spalding Inn*. It was soooo good! And Justin Drexler was totally amazing! He played Mr. Spalding's great-grandson. At the end of the movie, you find out . . . oh, I don't want to ruin it for you!"

"No, tell me!" I said. "You know scary movies and I don't mix. I'll never see it."

"Well, you find out that Justin's character is a ghost too! I had no idea the whole time . . . he's such a great actor, Sar! I think he might get nominated for an Oscar for his performance."

Justin Drexler was the guy Lily—and half my friends, to be honest—had a crush on. He was a pop star turned movie star.

"And look at how amazing-looking he is! He's even cuter with this new haircut!" Lily extended her phone to me. On the screen I could see a picture of a smiling guy with brown hair. He was definitely cute. Lily continued to gush. "And he has this great blog where he talks about all sorts of stuff, like what charities are important to him. I also read on his blog that he's writing a book! He's really into talking about how anyone can do anything they put their minds to. He's so positive! I can't wait for his book to come out!"

"Really?" Reading wasn't Lily's thing. I could finish

an entire book in the time it took her to daydream through the first page.

"I know, right?" Lily grinned.

Lily continued to talk about Justin and I did my best to listen, but I was a little preoccupied. My mind was on another guy. I tried to change the subject and hoped I wasn't being too obvious.

"So, Buddy's previous owners are coming for a visit soon, right?" I asked as I reached over to rub Buddy's belly. "When was that? And is that kid coming with them this time?"

"Who?"

Him. The boy with the white-blond hair. The boy with the piercing green eyes. The boy I couldn't stop thinking about.

"The grandkid. What's his name, Mason?" I asked. Of course I knew his name. I'd tattooed it on my brain ever since I saw his photo. Lily was forever crushing on celebrities like Justin Drexler, but I was crushing on a boy who wasn't famous. A boy I'd only seen in one picture. . . .